DATE DUE			
MAY 1 9 1995			

Fic
For   Forman, James D.
        Cry havoc

GAYLORD M2

CRY HAVOC

CRY
HAVOC

JAMES D. FORMAN

CHARLES SCRIBNER'S SONS

NEW YORK

This novel is a work of fiction. Names, characters, places, and incidents are either the product of the author's imagination or are used fictitiously. Any resemblance to actual persons, living or dead, is entirely coincidental.

Charles Scribner's Sons Books for Young Readers
Macmillan Publishing Company
866 Third Avenue, New York, NY 10022
Collier Macmillan Canada, Inc.

Printed in the United States of America
First Edition
10 9 8 7 6 5 4 3 2 1

Library of Congress Cataloging-in-Publication Data
Forman, James D.
Cry havoc / James D. Forman.—1st ed.
p. cm.
Summary: An Army experiment gone wrong unleashes upon a quiet village a group of large and vicious killer animals, and fifteen-year-old Cathy Cooper watches her world turn into a bloody nightmare.
ISBN 0-684-18838-4   [1. Horror stories.] I. Title.
PZ7.F76Cr   1988
[Fic]—dc19   87-37453
                                          CIP
                                          AC

A curse shall light upon the limbs of men.
Domestic fury and fierce civil strife
Shall cumber all the parts of Italy.
Blood and destruction shall be so in use,
And dreadful objects so familiar,
That mothers shall but smile when they behold
Their infants quarter'd with the hands of war.
All pity chok'd with custom of fell deeds.
And Caesar's spirit, ranging for revenge,
With Até by his side come hot from hell,
Shall in these confines with a monarch's voice
Cry "Havoc," and let slip the dogs of war.

Julius Caesar, ACT III, SCENE I

For all the loyal and steadfast dogs who have enriched my life:

Lassie, with the wise and knowing eyes
Penny, for sweetness of nature unexcelled
Joe, all zestful dog
Reveille, who always let us know
Taps, patient and uncomplaining
Tattoo, as beautiful as autumn
Annie, the streetwise orphan
Zephyr, the well traveled dog
Buckles, whose only demand is love

Directive 417-A

To: Department of Allocation and Assessment
Special Devices Research Center
Sandy Cliffs, New York

In reference to Report 237 regarding Research Grant 4387-J-1, Code Name: Cry Havoc:

Whereas it has been brought to the attention of this office that the subjects of the aforesaid genetic research grant have proven uniformly unstable, further investment in the program is to be terminated as of this date. Forthwith, the subjects of said program are to be eliminated with appropriate humane considerations, and any and all accumulated data, documentation, and research material, however peripheral, repeat, however peripheral, relevant to DNA, genetic manipulation, human or animal eugenics are to remain classified Top Secret and are to be sealed and returned by courier to this office.

General Lawrence T. Warden
Director, Office of Special Services and Research
The Pentagon
Washington, D.C.

November 3, 1988

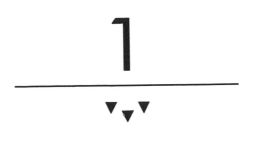

1

Heaven's blue streamed overhead on a balmy day of late Indian summer in the community of Sandy Cliffs, New York, on Long Island Sound. In the unseasonable warmth the buzzing of flies joined the lingering chorus of crickets. A dry west wind stripped a handful of brown leaves from the black walnut that flanked the first heavy thickets of blackberry and bittersweet. The leaves fell soundlessly into the dark bed of uncounted summers past or scaled the low bank of rhododendron to become a blemish on the lawn, meticulously maintained on a weekly basis by the Brothers Marino, gardeners to the affluent. A few leaves floated on the dark surface of the Lerners' swimming pool, oddly neglected now since Monica Lerner had begun seeing in nightmares their toddler son, Randy, floating face down. The Lerners were thinking of turning the pool next year into a huge sand box for Randy and his friends.

Inside the neocolonial house, which the Lerners had occupied since Henry's script had become a TV miniseries three years ago, Monica talked on the telephone while Randy lay asleep in a playpen on the fieldstone-and-slate terrace.

The dappling sun picked out points of light in the copper curls of the infant's hair. Then a late grasshopper wickered over the fieldstone wall and landed on the child's nose. Randy's eyes opened, and he protested with cries of surprising vehemence. The protest continued after the insect departed, becoming increasingly musical, experimental, only to be stoppered by a reflective thumb. The small hand moved on to explore a large kitchen spoon that deflected a ray of sun. Move the spoon and the blanket and the dazzle vanished; move it again and the mysterious fire returned. Randy laughed with delight.

At Monica Lerner's feet lay a large white poodle, which presently proceeded to the front door, waited patiently, scratched tentatively, and finally rumbled out a bark. Monica opened the door and the dog vanished, barking excitedly.

Her arrival on the terrace drew an instant cheer of delight from Randy. The threatening kitchen spoon caused the dog to wag a hesitant tail before continuing her rounds.

On his own rounds, Emilio Barbasso, the Mister Softee Ice Cream man, jingled his plaintive bell before the Lerner front door. Street peddling was strictly forbidden in Sandy Cliffs, but Emilio had his once-a-week regular customers. A cupid-faced, good-natured man with a quizzical, almost impertinent grin, Emilio loved children and ice cream unreservedly. He saw himself as an all-season Santa Claus bringing good cheer, and the bell he rang lustily tinkled in his own ears like sleigh bells.

While Emilio waited, his smile framed for the expected customer, Randy nursed his thumb again, fretting because nothing came from it. He beat the air with the kitchen spoon while casting reproachful glances at the door from which his mother seemed long overdue. His yearning for companionship was not long denied, but when it came it did so silently from the tangled, dark thickets beyond the rhododendrons, crossing the lawn as silent as a cloud shadow, scaling the fieldstone wall without a sound, as magical and charming an arrival to young Randy as the sudden sunlight on the spoon.

With a happy gurgling sound the toddler rose up on wobbly bowlegs to grasp the upper bar in one hand, the spoon in the other. His mouth, as toothless as a turtle's, broke into a broad grin. Tottering along the rail he shouted, "Bow wow!" The steel-gray eyes reflected back at him unwinking, a gaze neither furious nor apprehensive yet somehow as impassively menacing as the calm eye of a hurricane. Randy protruded his tongue invitingly and seized the new playmate by its upper lip, seeking to draw him closer.

In the broad, flat skull, the eyes narrowed, an effect strangely reptilian. Losing his hold, the baby toppled backward with a heartrending shriek, rolled over, bumped his head, lost the spoon. His transparent skin marbled out with irritation, and the spoon, recovered from the folds of the blanket, was brought down on his companion's nose, by no means a punishing blow, a mere flick that sent an imperceptible spark of static electricity from steel to brain. With that contact went a blind signal: "Enemy!" and "Now! Now!"

For an instant there was recognition, emotion that transcended the gap between species. Randy folded backwards into a sitting posture, his cheeks filled with surprise. Then there was the black engulfing fury, the baby briefly resisting, making himself hard and taut as a starfish, uttering a shrill of indignation before the deep snarl became muffled in flesh as fangs imbedded themselves, jolting left and right.

The jingle of the ice cream bell caused Monica to end her telephone conversation. The scream followed immediately, shrill, sexless, indescribable. It gave no clue to its import. Monica might have disregarded the noise entirely had it not emanated from the terrace where Randy had been napping. A surge of delinquent motherhood drove her down the corridor where the lolloping breeze blew out the blinds.

"Randy!" she exclaimed on throwing the door open. For a moment she stood transfixed, confused in a spinning world. The poodle slunk past her, or an apparition of that well-groomed pet, all smeared with red. Beyond the bespattered playpen Monica saw on the lawn what looked to her like a broken doll. She began to scream.

Emilio Barbasso froze midway through packing the inevitable quart tub of cherry twirl. He had heard a rabbit trill that way in a trap. A more feminine wail followed, intensified, until like some blind Medea the woman he had come to know only as Mrs. Lerner lurched through the screen door with something clutched in her arms. She shrieked at him, through him, wordlessly.

Emilio saw the world in terms of ice cream and for a bemused second he wondered, why would the woman clutch a melting blob of cherry twirl to her chest? And then, "Holy mother!" It was the child, and as Emilio watched, its limbs moved with an irrelevant vitality all their own. The tiny body jerked and shuddered as life tenaciously reentrenched itself.

By now Emilio was howling, too, howl after horrified howl until there was no breath left, and his cries subsided down the scale. Only then did he take action. With the woman pulled up beside him, blood and ice cream puddling the floor, he hurled his lurching van down Middle Island Road, right through the red traffic light there and all the rest of the traffic lights, red or green, until he made the swinging turn into St. Jude Hospital. Throughout that seemingly endless race his passenger rocked the torn infant in her arms as though her loving might restore it to laughter. Too late. Blood no longer gushed from the small body. The pump had mercifully stopped.

2

▼▼▼
▼

James Cooper, aged forty-two, and younger looking except around the eyes, drove from his law office at the county seat, Mohegan. He would presently meet his perplexing daughter, Catherine, at the railroad station in Port Monroe, the nearest commuter terminal to Sandy Cliffs. He wore an unobtrusive Brooks Brothers gray suit and drove a new dark green Buick. At thirty, he had known where he was going, but now, having shifted his cargo of guilt, puzzlement, and frustration into another generation, Jim Cooper could glance back upon a not entirely golden youth and forward to narrowing prospects and cold decrepitude.

Forty years squandered. He would never scale the Alps with a troop of elephants, never found a great city, or discover the headwaters of the Amazon, yet Jim Cooper knew he was respected in the community for his untiring efforts to make Sandy Cliffs a "better place" and feared in court by opposing witnesses, where his dark, penetrating stare and drooping piratical moustache were becoming legend. Jim himself attributed his measure of success to his father's forceful steering. The older man had always marked Jim's growing on the bedroom door, and this kind of pressure had seen him through Berkshire Academy, a family tradition, as was Princeton University and Columbia Law School, and on into the role of tireless attorney, dogged in argument, persuasive, impervious to counter logic.

Though not such a rock-ribbed Republican as his grandfather, Judge Aberdeen Cooper, Jim had not been able to throw out that old man's prized possession, a portrait of Franklin D. Roosevelt framed in a mahogany toilet seat. This dubious artifact had, in the judge's opinion, signified that president's responsibility for sending the good old days of rugged Americanism down the drain. The portrait had long been retired to the attic, where Jim smiled at it occasionally, wondering what old Aberdeen would think of his grandson now. Of the judge's goals, Jim had fallen sadly short professionally. As a family man, Lord knows, he had achieved disaster: a mentally shattered wife, Joan, and a troubled daughter, Catherine.

As her mother's illness grew worse, Cathy had been sent away to boarding school, first to Ethel Walker, where she had skipped a grade, then to Jim's own Berkshire Academy, now coeducational, where she increasingly complained of the teachers, the food, and the difficulty of making friends. Her grades had declined and finally plummeted. There had been a confrontation with a teacher and now she was on her way home, suspended, charged with a nonscholarly attitude following an ugly scene with the headmaster when a little kowtowing might have paid off.

9

Cathy needed strong steering, and Jim dared not fail as he had failed with his wife. Just how he had failed, he could not say. His wife's problems had quickly passed beyond the expertise of a layman. Joan was still loaded with talent and love, but the world had simply frightened her nearly to death. Looking back, Jim blamed himself for retreating into his work, for being too remote by nature. But all along he had encouraged Joan's poetry, let her pour thousands into her dog kennel venture, uncomplainingly purchased her paints, pastels, and drawing paper after she had become afraid to drive a car. And he had spared no medical expense. Nine years had gone by, nine years since their anniversary weekend when Joan had tried suicide and done that ghastly business with the puppies. Nine years of scribbling with crayons on the walls of her room in an institution because life outside was too much to handle.

Control. That had always been Jim's answer, drummed into him by his father and grandfather. Keep things under control. Make them happen, stick to goals. Man was never designed to bask on a tropic beach waiting for the coconuts to fall. That was the weak way out, to go and live in nature with the sun and waves far from human conflict. Once upon a time that might have worked, but it was too late for hiding now. The modern world was at your throat, and Jim Cooper had been taught to meet it head on. He clung to this with a mingled sense of a job well done at the office and a feeling of love, hope, and despair where his home life was concerned.

Though Jim regarded Joan as irretrievably lost, he would go to hell and back before he would allow the same thing to happen to his daughter. Such was his preoccupation that he almost failed to brake for a Mister Softee Ice Cream van

10

that without signaling screeched across lanes and up the drive to St. Jude's. A police car made the turn behind it. I was damn near dead, Jim reflected. That idiot would never have stopped. You'd think he'd have had enough respect for humanity to toll his ice cream bell. Shaken, Jim drove along more slowly. What was happening to human caring and responsibility? Deep down he felt the fear of one who lives in a world not made for him, whose own world is sifting away, vanishing beyond recall.

Turning onto Port Monroe's Main Street, he wondered what had happened to the cherry trees, cut down so long ago for parking he almost forgot to miss them. Port Monroe was the end of the line. Here the commuters got off and the trains went back to Manhattan. When his grandfather had traveled to New York City only three cars spent the day at the railroad station. Now it took three huge, metered lots to hold them.

Cathy's train was late. Jim leaned on the wheel, sang in a nasal voice, "I'd rather be dead than let a steam drill beat me down, Lord, Lord." This was sung with real conviction though he had never laid hands on a steam drill, or a ten-pound hammer for that matter.

Jim locked the car, walked through the station with its aura of old men, spent cigars, and urine, and climbed onto the empty platform. Around him was the distant clamor of rush hour. An unseen horizon hummed with mechanized life. The empty tracks glowed like neon in the evening light as they narrowed under the Sprucedale bridge and curved west. On a still day he could hear the train clanging out of the next station to the west, gathering speed. It was a sound that made him shiver, for trains had always been for Jim the lonely agents of parting and separation.

11

Finally like a great worm with a blazing eye the local out of Pennsylvania Station eased under the Sprucedale Bridge, seemed to grow in size rather than proximity. At the last Jim stepped away from the iron bumper, which had crumpled some years before when a train had kept on going through the old station and into the street. The train shuddered to a stop, trembling like a huge dreaming dog. A conductor swung down, followed by the commuters, who walked fast, determined to enjoy their weekend reprieve. The crowd quickly thinned. Jim began to wonder if Cathy had pulled one of her tricks.

Then he saw her, blond, well put together, long of leg with narrow hips and square, thin shoulders. Despite a bulky suitcase, she walked with the gait of one who liked to be out of doors walking every day. Jim was inclined to think: good work, human race, all that energy and vigor. She had flashed so fast from childhood into adolescence, soon womanhood. He could not catch hold of anything that changed shape so swiftly. It seemed as though he had to revise each idea about his daughter as soon as it was formulated. At least she still wore the old blue jeans embroidered with small Disney creatures with big eyes. Yet there was a wildness about her, not of mania or insanity, but rather a wildness of nature and innocence. It was the wildness he sensed in the seagull's call, an ability to ride out the storm instinctively. God knows he hoped so, for they were certainly in for stormy weather.

Innocent or not, Catherine Cooper had been suspended from prep school. On the one hand, it was a disgrace; on the other, just what she wanted. To hell with boarding school, any boarding school. The autumn term had been a bad one, engraving a line of bewilderment between her large, clear blue eyes and encircling them with a faint brown smudge of weariness. She expected an immediate outburst from her father, and despite her own inner struggle she was ready for battle if cornered.

As Jim came forward to grasp her suitcase, Catherine adjusted her face to a smile of dutiful greeting.

"Well, Cat, how are you?" he asked.

She took the Cat as a favorable sign. It was a pet name going way back. Usually it was Cathy, Catherine only in moments of stress.

"Home rather early for the holidays, I'd say."

"Just couldn't wait, Dad," she returned in a clear, cool voice, then emphasized the joke with a "Ha, ha" of false laughter. They walked side by side to the car. "Have I changed a whole lot, do you think?"

"In less than two months?" he replied, though he had noticed a subtle range of new expressions suggesting advancing maturity. That could mean trouble. "Is that a new laugh?"

"Is it?" Cathy replied, convinced her father was determined to have the sort of heart-to-heart she was anxious to avoid.

"I think yes, a bit deeper." He started the car.

She tried a diversion. "Dad, did you hear about the baby that was eaten by the family poodle?"

"Is this a sick joke, or what?" he asked.

"I'm serious. On the train, this kid had a radio. It just happened in Sandy Cliffs, right near us. The poodle's dead, too."

3

▼▼▼

As Jim and Cathy Cooper turned left off Main Street heading for home, Private Lance Hagedorn was patrolling the perimeter fence of the Army Special Devices Research Center in Sandy Cliffs. It was a routine task, quite pleasant on a mild autumn afternoon. When Project Cry Havoc had first been contemplated, an electrified fence carrying a sublethal charge had been authorized. Subsequently, due to the expense and in the interest of better community relations, the original cyclone-style steel-link fence had simply been raised from six to eight feet with a double strand of barbed wire on top and an alarm bell that would ring in the front office in the event of tampering.

The alarm system had been triggered a few days before, but with the Cry Havoc project aborted, the search had been given low priority. Private Hagedorn had been out looking for breaks in the fence before, all false alarms, and except for one dose of poison ivy, he regarded the duty as a nature walk. The gaping hole that he found this time came as a surprise. The area was officially mapped as B7, about fifty feet from the eroded sand cliff with its narrow beach below and an equal distance from where the wire made a turn inland to separate the unimproved grounds of the Center from the remains of an abandoned farm that had not yet been picked up for development.

Private Hagedorn scrutinized the damage with a flashlight, as dark was coming on. Vandalism, probably; hoodlums on those big balloon-tired, gas-powered tricycles had been playing hell with the sand dunes in the bird sanctuary. The village police never seemed to run them down. One might just have butted on through the fence for the hell of it. But then why did the wire seem to have been forced outward? And there was a crispness to the hole that suggested wire cutters. Whatever rust he could see was fresh, granular, and orange.

Private Hagedorn wrote all this down carefully on a notepad, not knowing whether this hole had set off the alarm. No doubt he'd be handed a spool of patching wire as usual, and that would be the end of it.

4

Traffic whizzed by. It took the Coopers a long time to make the left-hand turn onto Middle Island Road. By now the sun was an orange glare in the west. Glancing at her father, hunched in silhouette over the wheel, it occurred to Cathy that he was getting old. He reminded her of a tall marsh bird in bleak weather.

"How are my dog friends?" she asked as they waited in traffic at the Harbor View light.

"Getting sand and hair all over the house as usual. Taps'll be in heat before you know it. I should have had her spayed years ago. It should have been done to the first bitch we brought home."

"Dad, that wouldn't have helped. The dogs are about the best thing that ever happened to us—well, you know, as a family." Those had been happy times, when the kennel still had promise and her mother still had hope. Feeding, walking, grooming, and training dogs seemed to take up Joan's entire day. At bedtime there had been reading, Mom reciting that corny poem about a dog's unflinching devotion to his human family. How did it go? "Ah, what was then Llewelyn's pain! For now the truth was clear: His gallant hound the wolf had slain, to save Llewelyn's heir."

"It seems like such a long time ago," Cathy mused aloud.

"Oh, kiddo," Jim replied, "if only you knew the half of it."

Ten years of therapy and self-pity had left Joan as miserable now as she had been in the beginning. How many times had he heard her say, "Why was I ever made alive?" All those years—guilt, suffering, and money—and there was not much he could do about it except get a divorce and make her more unhappy.

"If I were home more often," Cathy said, "I'd get the kennel back in shape."

Over my dead body, flashed through Jim's mind, but realizing Cathy was looking for enthusiasm he said instead, "Well, that's an idea. But frankly, Cat, I think it's more people-breeding we need."

"The Master Race, Dad? *Sieg Heil* and all that?"

"Kiddo, I'm no Hitler, but not every idea is bad because a bad man believed it. Human population's out of control. We've got to prune it back somehow, or pay an awful price."

"Is that why you like those iddy-biddy tree things of yours?" Cathy asked. She referred to the bonsai trees introduced into the household by the Vietnamese couple, the Nuncs, who came in twice a week to clean the house. Jim found the trees fascinating and admitted it: the tiny Japanese maple even now in crimson leaf, the weatherbeaten

17

little Chinese juniper he'd been told could live for centuries, the pyracantha with its orange berries, and the pink azalea that bloomed in spring. Imagine controlling natural development like that. What a work of art!

"They really are beautifully controlled little things," Jim said.

"The trees or the Nuncs?" Cathy asked with scornful amusement.

"Both, damn it. The place would be a dump without the Nuncs, and you know it."

They drove in silence past the high school. The grandstand stood out bare and black. The first house lights were coming on.

"I suppose you're picking up Mom tomorrow for Thanksgiving dinner and all," Cathy said.

"She's home already," Jim replied. "I got her yesterday."

Oh, Lord, thought Cathy. Not even a day's grace. She had a vision of her mother peeping from behind a door into a dark hallway.

"Then I suppose Miss Huntington is in residence, too." Cathy's voice was cold.

"Correct," Jim admitted. "She used to be your Aunt Pat."

"Ah, Pa-tri-cia," Cathy intoned, syllable by syllable. "Soon Sandy Cliffs will resound with the sound of music."

Jim frowned but made no comment. Pat Huntington, a college friend of Joan's, had remained a steadfast visitor over the years despite a promising career in opera, always promising—good reviews in Brazil, Czechoslovakia, cool approval at La Scala—never quite the diva. She had the voice, was a fine, sensitive actress, but she lacked the claws necessary to scale the heights.

18

"We'll all have to make a big effort to have a good time for your mother's sake," Jim pleaded. No response. "Isn't it your turn to say something, kiddo?"

"Why Pat?"

"Because she's your mom's closest friend and she's been a big help to me. I even think she might still spark your mother's old enthusiasm."

"I just bet," Cathy said scornfully, suspicious.

"That I'm having an affair with your mom's old roommate from Vassar?"

"You said it, Dad."

"Now don't be childish."

"Now don't be childish," Cathy mimicked. "What do you expect me to think?"

"Maybe you're just giving me ideas. Even an attorney is an honest man now and then."

"Dad, I don't need all this."

"Cat, in some circles it wouldn't be to my credit, but I've never cheated on your mother. Believe it or not, I still love her. While we're on the subject of true romance, what about you and Bruce? Don't you think our master mariner is a bit elderly?"

"Elderly?"

"For you, I mean." Jim added, not so much concerned with the age difference as what he understood to be Bruce's goal in life: reconditioning an old sailboat in which to enjoy the endless summer of the West Indies, with an occasional charter party when food ran out or the hull needed paint.

"Come on, Dad." Cathy protested. Bruce Stewart was a freshman in college and had been her club sailing instructor the summer before. "Three whole years, Dad. What's three years?"

"Maybe I mean you're a bit young."

19

Cathy was on her guard. "You used to like Bruce."

"I still do. I always have," Jim admitted, thinking at the same time that there was something curiously unfinished about the boy, an eagerness that properly belonged to extreme youth. Bruce also had a well-bred aversion to all forms of profitable labor. "I could wish he were, well, more seriously motivated."

"He knows how to have fun," Cathy said defensively.

"And is he so important to you?"

"Of course," she replied, deadpan, "I'm after his money."

"For your information, if I know Bruce's old man, Bruce may never get a red cent."

"There's some kind of trust fund," Cathy explained with superior knowledge. "Bruce can afford to take his time and find out what he likes."

"As long as what he likes ends up being productive. Believe me, Cat, I want you kids to have a good time," Jim said gently. "But people who have that primarily in mind don't usually achieve it."

Cathy had been through this one before: education to provide the tools to control one's environment, or at least hold it off, like the jungle. She got on better with her father during those seasons of benevolent neglect than when he showered her with concern.

She might have said, "Just what use is an education when you expect to go gaga in a few years?" But that would be going for the throat and was more than she wanted to put into words. Instead she jumped ahead in their usual argument and said, "Be a lawyer. Right, Dad?"

"If we're talking about you, Cat, I'm not content with your being a lawyer. I want a judge, the first woman judge in this family. Now we're talking ambition."

The mood was still genial, but Cathy watched her father's face as if they were fencing with foils. She thought of Bruce's easy good nature. He didn't see the world as a jungle, needed no weapons. If Bruce had his way, life would be one long holiday.

To their left was the Sandy Cliffs Golf Club. It had been laid out in the 1920s complete with a polo field for Harrimans and Hitchcocks. Now all that glamor was gone, and the club had opened its rolls to anyone who could pay the fee.

Beyond the golf course were the empty paddocks of the old Gould estate, part of which had been taken over by the Army's Special Devices Research Center. Experiments, real and rumored, from radar to nerve gas and gene splicing, had been conducted over the years since the beginning of the second world war. Now the gossip mill said the place was to be taken over by the county and turned into public parkland.

"Penny for your thoughts," Jim said.

"Not worth it," Cathy replied. Jim might have explored this, but for the lights of two parked police cars, their rotating beacons sending signals of distress. An officer leaned against one car, talking into his radio. Occasionally he lifted a distracted face to gaze at a nearby house—the Lerner house, though Jim did not know it. His father could have named all the families in Sandy Cliffs, mostly founding members of the Golf Club. Now, with the population explosion, Jim's neighbors had become strangers.

"I bet that's the place," Cathy said.

Jim was puzzled. "What place?"

"Where the kid was eaten."

"What a ghoulish speculation," Jim replied. "Still, I suppose it puts our layabout cops on their toes."

Sandy Cliffs was unusual in that it had maintained a private police force since 1904 when a one-man night patrol had been hired. Now, despite county willingness to take over, there were sixteen men in the village force and a proposal at the village hall to up this to twenty. With the exception of an occasional unsolved burglary and one motorcycle flasher who had astonished the summer beachgoers with his dexterity, the force limited itself to traffic control at cocktail parties, bar mitzvahs, and weddings, returning lost pets, and ticketing village cars. They listened now and then to the city police radio, to crimes and alarms and drug busts in the big town. This week the blotter in Sandy Cliffs showed only one case of accidental trespass and an illegal bonfire gone out of control. Now they had death by violence, and the police were not quite sure what to do about it. At least they could guard the house, protect the Lerners' property and privacy.

A half mile farther on, Jim turned into Woodside. At one time the whole street had belonged to his grandfather. Gradually most of the area had been sold and developed, with Jim inheriting the original Cooper house, built in the 1920s, and four acres around it. He could remember driving golf balls on his grandfather's front lawn, and shooting a .22 in any direction he chose. Now everywhere there weren't houses there were plans for houses, and a little autumn leaf burning resulted in a visit from the fire department, courtesy of a vigilant neighbor. Yes, the tanglewoods of his childhood were vanishing.

They would be home in minutes.

"Let's sign a truce, you and me, Cathy. Let's concentrate on coping with your mom. I know it's hard."

"I don't know how to act with her," Cathy admitted, sounding more the little girl than she liked to.

"Just remember she loves you, kiddo. That may be a nuisance, but she does. It's been months, and it'll be months until next time. Well, Christmas, anyway. Just don't say anything you'll regret. When she's gone, we'll straighten out the school mess."

"Don't you mean you'll straighten me out, Dad?"

"I didn't say that. Cat, we're nearly there. I'm not up to a browbeating right now. Just try to smile, please. And remember, your mother wants Pat here. She asked her to come. Frankly, I don't know what I'd do without Pat's help. I can't seem to count on much from you. Honest to God, Cat, sometimes you act like you hate Joan and me."

"Don't listen to me," she whispered. "I love you, both of you." There were tears in her eyes now. "But I'm scared."

Jim slowed the car to a near stop at the head of the drive. "Why, Cath?" She made no answer. "Why?"

"I'm afraid of her suffering."

"Cat, honestly . . ."

"Just let me finish, please, Dad. Okay?" She took a long shuddering breath. "I'm scared of getting sick like that."

"You won't," Jim insisted with more vehemence than he felt. "We'll talk. I promise we'll talk about it later. Right now they're waiting."

Although sunset lingered in the sky, the lights of the Cooper home glowed up ahead. Jim let the car roll on. Behind the kitchen the kennel was dark. Cathy knew the paint was flaking, the wire rusty, the wood porous with termites and decay. Culloden Kennels, her mother had called it in the little ad she'd run in the Kennel Club magazine in the hope her love for dogs could pay its way. When Cathy had remarked, "What a funny name," her mother had laughed, saying, "My side of the family came from Scotland, and Scots have a passion for lost causes." Now

Cathy could see the two dogs, Taps and Reveille, standing erect, forepaws against the kennel fence. Their greeting rose sharp on the autumn air, a call of loyalty and love that vibrated down the years since humans had cowered in caves, armed with chipped stones against the dark.

As Jim pulled the suitcase from the trunk he asked, "You okay, Cat?" She nodded. "It's good to have you here."

"Then it's great to be home," she told him, walking not to the door but to the kennel.

5

▼ ▼
  ▼

The two shepherds thrust black muzzles up against the kennel gate in a frenzy of welcome. Their jaws quivered lightly before they broke into a chorus of joyful barks. Cathy flung open the gate and the pair, grinning from ear to ear, danced out, nearly bowling her over. She laughed, hugged each dog. For an unrestrained moment Cathy felt she could live her life with animals.

"I suppose they have to come in now," Jim said, unguarded affection in his voice.

Joan stood in the front hall. A step behind her, imposing as Pallas Athena, stood Pat Huntington. She seemed, as the door opened, to be urging Joan forward.

It had always been hard for Cathy to be physically demonstrative with her mother. Now she managed to embrace Joan with cautious enthusiasm. She had never felt so many bones and angles. The two stepped apart, holding hands. Joan gazed at her daughter through tinted glasses as if her life depended on the unswerving steadiness of her gaze. There was much of the mirror image about these two: good athletic frame, long blond hair, fine features, but where Cathy had the pink-and-white bloom of youth, Joan had gazed too long into the fire. It had left her withered and dry beyond her forty-one years. She might have been one of Edgar Allan Poe's heroines, doomed to consumption and an early grave.

"Mom, how great you're home!" Cathy exclaimed.

"I should hope so, being home for Thanksgiving. And seeing all of you. It really is you, Cathy, isn't it? You're not a nurse dressed up to look like you?"

"Of course not, Mom." Cathy gave a nervous laugh. "What an idea." She was not sure if her mother was kidding. Her hands slipped away from Joan's as she wondered how such pale, thin hands could feel hot instead of cold. About her mother clung a sharp, medicinal smell.

"Mom," she said, "you look great," thinking her mother must have lost another ten pounds. She fought an overwhelming desire to be very distant and quiet, as if on a cloud.

Pat took Cathy's arm with a pressure of reassurance. "Not to worry, we'll have a fine time," she said, the very words to set Cathy's nerves on edge. "We've all been looking forward to having you home for the holidays." Her voice was totally sincere, full of music and range, what Cathy thought of as a "stage" voice. Sometimes it dropped so low Cathy imagined her playing boys' games as a child. Lively lights flickered in her eyes.

Pat wore no jewelry, and no makeup stained her flawless complexion. For her, beauty was simply good theater, and she resorted to cosmetics only when necessary, applying them with careful disdain. Tonight her dress was white and unadorned, her auburn hair exceptionally long and on this occasion braided down her back. Pat was too old to wear it so, but Cathy had to admit grudgingly it was a splendid adornment. She was reminded of a figure from a romantic revival painting signifying purity. Only Pat's big capable hands did not suit the image. Not only were they as large and hard as a man's, they were distinctly pink, those of a compulsive washer, which said something, Cathy wasn't sure what, but it did suggest a concealed vulnerability.

Already the reunion seemed to be running out of steam, though Jim had embraced his wife and bestowed on Pat's cheek a kiss more domestic than romantic. Only the dogs seemed unreservedly enthusiastic: Reveille, the big sleepy-eyed male, and Taps, the female, a year younger with a muzzle that seemed too narrow to contain a full set of teeth. Both grinned horribly with enthusiasm, whimpering in typical doggy confusion of feelings in which excitement and boredom were thoroughly mixed.

Reveille watched his people, his pack, with puzzled interest. His long tail made uncertain conversation. Presently he vanished, returning with an old tennis ball, which he dropped before Cathy for prideful inspection. She bent to pick it up and he put his muzzle up to her ear as though he had a vital secret to impart.

"You want a walk. So do I," Cathy whispered.

Then the dog beat the floor with his tail. Taps joined the pleading, began to bark.

"Bad dogs!" Jim admonished them.

At those dread words the pair laid back their ears against their skulls, crouching, chins to floor. Only the disgraced tails moved hopefully, anticipating a reprieve.

"Anyone else care for a stroll with the dogs?" Cathy asked. She needed the fresh air.

There were no takers. Pat laughed merrily (Cathy suspected she was putting it on) but declined, since someone had to get supper. Joan seemed distressed by the prospect, saying it had been a tiring day. What had happened to her old love of dogs, Cathy wondered.

"Don't be long," Jim said. "It's nearly dark, Cat."

Cathy was ashamed of her own eagerness to be out of the house, away from them all. Step aside, she thought, make way for the crazed adolescent who is showing the first signs of mania, delusions, whatever. She simply had to get a breather, and the dogs were the excuse.

Once outside, it seemed only the weight of her Reeboks held her to the ground. Otherwise gravity would fail; up, up and away. What remained of the sun smoldered in the western haze of city pollution. She felt the autumn chill as they headed down toward the meadow and Long Island Sound, the dogs trooping on ahead, alert for rabbits, for anything that moved.

Cathy could scarcely imagine walking without the companionship of dogs—dogs wise and foolish, funny and sad, blustery and street-wise, knocking over garbage cans, nipping mailmen, barking at phantoms. Now loose on the lane they seemed like self-important emissaries bent on missions that in some fashion kept the neighborhood running. She knew the neighbors' dogs better than the neighbors, liked them better, too, on principle, except for one high-pitched little sausage dog that seemed not to run so much as flop about like a toad.

Funny how much dogs seemed to be the mirror image of their masters. Some snarled and laid back their ears in instant suspicion while others were immediately trusting and lovable, projecting some part of their owner's inner benevolence and optimism. Maybe that was why she liked Bruce—for his positive canine qualities, his happiness in the present, the absence of dark forebodings.

Cathy and the dogs headed down the wooded hill as they had so many times before. A fresh November wind with crisp, cold fingers ruffled her hair, but it was still a friendly cold without sharp nails. The bird sanctuary beyond was a shattered lake of gold from which the meadow grass seemed a leaping fire. She missed the summer egrets, the ducks. Even the solitary pair of swans had vanished.

When a gray heron rose with majestic wings over the distant ridge of dunes, the dogs joined in a halfhearted chase. Cathy's thoughts lingered far behind—school problems, arguments unresolved, and especially her mother and the terror that her own problems, thriving in inherited genes, might doom her to a similar fate.

Cathy shivered more from her reflections than the evening's chill. Her mother's doctors had assured her that there was no hereditary link. Cathy sensed that deep inside herself there was a coil of most resilient steel, and yet. . . . She crossed the meadow bridge. It had been wooden in the old days and subject to winter storms. It was concrete now. She and Bruce had put their initials in the wet cement over a year ago. The initials made her smile, and then she found herself listening. Was it just a tonal change in the tidal water? She paused briefly, her head lifted like a foal listening for strangeness. The shepherds froze stiffly, too, in that posture that with hunting dogs is referred to as "dead set," when their every attention is fixed on the quarry. Then something blurred upward with a shrill, witchlike cry. Cathy drew in her breath, then relaxed; it was only a pheasant, more alarmed than she.

She walked on, trying to set things in order. She knew most of the story, how her parents had met on a tennis court during their sophomore year in college. Joan had been blond, fit, and sunburned, dreaming of France. They had not become serious until her return from Europe. Marriage had followed upon Jim's graduation from law school. With his practice established, there had been the delayed but often warmly recalled honeymoon in East Africa. Soon thereafter Cathy had joined the family. By then the change in Joan had already begun. You weren't supposed to say nervous breakdown any more. Her dad avoided the phrase, though it seemed to fit the amorphous nature of what afflicted her mother. Joan never defamed the neighbors or suspected them of tunneling beneath the house with explosives. At first she had accused Jim of callous neglect but never imagined him seasoning the salad with arsenic. Occasionally she sunbathed without a bra in the closed privacy of the back yard but never relied on invisibility to dance naked at cocktail parties. Cathy knew of her insomnia, the early waking, tears before dawn, the inability to laugh or accept anything new or different.

All this had led to a psychiatrist, then a private institution at about three thousand dollars a month. "We can't afford it," Joan had said, though Jim never told her the cost. She knew, all right, but had stayed there for almost two years after a doctor had assured Jim that the first months were critical, a cure within a year vital. After that the odds against recovery soared astronomically.

Other private institutions followed. Reluctantly Jim had arranged a brief intensive treatment at Northland Hospital.

Undernourishment and her refusal to eat led to tube feedings, massive doses of vitamins, a battery of drugs: Lithium Carbonate, Thorazine, Parnate, plus a brief experiment in old-fashioned coma therapy. Joan had become terrified of the technicians and after a month she had been released as cured, with a caution to Jim that he keep a close eye on his wife since a relapse into depression was often associated with suicide.

What came next remained vague in Cathy's recollection. She had been gotten out of the way into summer camp, returning to find her mother a volunteer admission into Brightsides, a place of run-down red brick buildings amid thick trees. The puppies had all been sold, the kennel closed, and since then the status of the Cooper family had changed little except that her mother's visits were becoming more frequent.

By now the sun lay below the horizon, its last shafts of light cold as the moon's. It would soon be night. Pink clouds edged with gold still drifted over the hills of Westchester. They were turning purple. It was the hour when bats fly low. As Cathy neared the dunes she heard the waves beyond and inhaled deeply: low tide, a smell you had to grow up with to love.

Might things have gone differently had she been home that summer? A six year old? Not likely, but it troubled her that so much had changed while she was away at camp. She still wondered if it might not relate to her father's pushiness, his nitpicking criticisms of Joan's domestic shortcomings, his virtual bullying her into piano lessons, for which she had no aptitude, and the garden club, when all Joan wanted to do was paint. Cathy could still recall her mother replying in a tremulous voice, "Jim, I'm sorry, I'm not an ideal suburban wife," with her father doggedly insisting, "Well, then, let's work on it. Let's see what we can do." At the time her mother's face had distressed Cathy. Now, half amused, she pictured Jim as some kind of well-intentioned Doctor Frankenstein, the molder of the women in his life.

Hands thrust into jeans pockets and bunched into fists, Cathy waded behind the dogs through the soft sand dunes. The tide was out. A sandbar seeded with mussel shells gleamed above the ebb. Gusts of wind fretted the water into bronze scales. A jet swam overhead on its long western glide to where the canopy of city lights pulsed upward, brilliant as the Milky Way.

Somewhere a dog raised a lonely territorial howl. Far off another answered, a pure, silvery bugle call. Realizing it was the season when summer tenants left their pets behind, Cathy could feel the rootlets of every hair. She knew that kind of loneliness.

In that uncertain moment, when twilight seemed to linger though night had already fallen, she might have taken the short course west to Kidd's rocks where North Creek emptied into the Sound. Some said the huge house on the point there was the model for Daisy's place in *The Great Gatsby*. Cathy chose the longer, darker course, following the high-tide line, a strip of seaweed, driftwood, and beer cans, eastward toward the eroded bluffs that bore the Special Devices Research Center. She could see the turrets of the Gould mansion etched black on the horizon above the trees.

What happened to girls who craved long, lonely walks, she wondered. High up, barely visible now, seagulls floated on motionless wings. Their cries were eerie and restless. Solitude had brought no illuminations. Her mother had walked at night, sometimes all night. The comparison frightened her. She determined to get hold of herself and stepped out firmly, being transformed as she went, appearing more self-assured at every step. By now a yellow curved blade of an autumn moon rode above the Gould mansion. In the sleeping meadow she seemed to see shadowy forms among the bayberry and beach plum thickets.

Following the dogs, Cathy was now opposite what remained of the old Van Rath orchard and farm. Up in there was the farmhouse, overgrown with bittersweet and Virginia creeper. The two dogs had halted, pointing that way as though signaling game. Cathy found this disquieting. In most older communities there is at least one decrepit house rumored to be haunted as a result of some unnatural act or unexplained death. Such was the Van Rath farm, and if half the stories were believed as earnestly as they were reported, there would be no likelihood of trespassers. Children claimed to have seen light from a garret window or heard inhuman sounds from the cellar. Older, bolder boys who rode through the overgrown yard on minibikes reported that climbing roses blooming on the sagging porch struck dead those bees that sought their nectar.

Unlike most such tales, behind these stories was a grim reality. Cathy had heard it from her father, who had been involved in the case. The Van Raths, Sandy Cliff's last real farmers, had produced one son, a loner, drafted into the war in Vietnam from whence he had been dishonorably discharged for cruelty to prisoners. Once home, he had failed in every job he tried until, after a boatyard in Port Monroe was torched, he had been arrested, tried, and acquitted on a charge of arson. Subsequently he had vanished just as his parents were found dead in their kitchen, the gas stove left on. Accident or double suicide? The coroner had chosen the former. They were good Catholics, after all. But there had been hints of murder, with their vanished son the prime suspect.

Cathy found the place tempting, thrillingly so. What if he had returned, the lunatic son, and waited inside like a spider in a web for her to slowly open the door? No, the place was undoubtedly teeming with snakes. With a quick pulse beating in her ears, *dum de dum, dum de dum,* she turned suddenly for home.

As she walked even faster now, the vast blackness of the evening seemed to enlarge itself around her. Now that she had let apprehension in, she felt watched, stalked. Cautiously she paused to listen. There was the rapid pulse beat and beyond that a sort of double awareness, not just waves or the creep of the tide but something else, a sound that the night makes, a faint movement quite close. Someone was near.

At this point Cathy saw in the poor light, or imagined that she saw, a print at her feet, and then another, leading off toward the shore. They were too differentiated to be that of a horse, and yet were that large. Tiny beads of perspiration formed on her upper lip. As Cathy scanned the horizon she felt sure someone was staring back at her. Something unseen seemed to be growing while she diminished until she had to move to break the spell.

The dogs were far ahead and Cathy began to jog. Having given way to flight, all manner of creatures stirred around her: shaggy forms with bony, almost-human faces, heavily bearded, their evil eyes glimmering, moving not on four legs but six. Her mouth had turned glutinous and bitter. She was running full out now, the dogs loping along, delighted. Panting, Cathy found herself remembering the games of hide-and-seek at camp, the nervous delights of running away, the slow count until the seeker shouted, "Here I come! Ready or not!"

She pounded over the meadow bridge. It was too dark now to make out the initials, but the road was pale in the moonlight. Nothing behind, she felt sure of that. Only a trail of scent marked their return. But from the tall thickets on either side a tiger might have lurked unseen to launch itself at her jugular.

She felt more at ease with the bridge behind her. Up ahead, as though cheering her on, were the last crickets under the trees. How foolish, she told herself. I won't panic like this again. Under the first trees she was still breathing hard. I scarcely know what I was afraid of to begin with. Only a small inner voice whispered in reply: *Exactly what you'll be afraid of next time.* She could see the lights of home, bright and welcoming.

They went the rest of the way slowly, the dogs walking on either side as though on leashes. From beyond the tidal stream that fed the bird sanctuary, they had been observed, not so much seen as heard and deeply inhaled, examined, and stored away in memory by ears that were sensitive as radar, by a nose that could pick up the faintest odors, assess, and record them with the flawless speed of a computer.

6

Thanksgiving Day in the kitchen: the Cooper turkey browned in the oven and the Macy's parade filled the television screen. Cathy looked up occasionally from rolling pie dough. A news flash showed French farmers pouring out tubs of nuclear-contaminated milk. A clip on the Lerner tragedy, as it was now being called, followed. The policeman who had shot the family poodle was interviewed. "No," he said, "if you mean the dog, he just stood there with his tail between his legs." Question: "And then you shot him?" "Yes, blew his brains out." At this point the reporter explained that Mr. Lerner, overcome by grief, had attacked the carcass with a baseball bat. Then the driver of the ice cream truck was questioned. Shy on camera, he said only, "It was awful. Just like Nam."

"Nam," echoed Jim. "I damn near burned my draft card at Columbia, and I was too nearsighted to go anyway. Now we have meltdowns. No more passenger pigeons, no more dinosaurs, no more saber-toothed tigers. We're lucky to still be around."

Cathy smiled blandly at her father. He was raving again. The state of the world in general did not alarm her—it was too remote, not like her mother—and her father's ranting seemed only a smoke screen to conceal what was in the air, a sense of things coming that could not be avoided.

On the television a huge Dumbo balloon filled the screen. Then came Little Red Riding Hood with her arm around the shoulders of a toothy, beaming wolf.

Cathy concentrated on the preparations for Thanksgiving dinner. The Cooper family had always loved food. Cookbooks were never thrown out. Recipes from generations back, many now food-stained and indecipherable, were squirreled away in a tin box. In moments of stability much devotion had been bestowed upon the preparation of meals, undoubtedly because such occasions had become increasingly rare. Cathy and Jim had come to rely almost entirely upon take-out and the microwave except when Pat was visiting. Pat seemed to have more aptitude for cooking than she liked to admit, saying only that her mother had been a gourmet cook and maybe some of it had rubbed off. This was all Cathy knew about Pat's mother, except that she had kept a spotless house, which she had cleaned twice a day right up until the eve of her unexpected death. Pat had been a teenager at the time, but she had run the household thereafter until she had gone away to college. This had proved a welcome escape, just why Cathy could only speculate, and she had rarely returned to Oklahoma where her father still lived and was a member of Alcoholics Anonymous. Was that the clue?

The dogs strolled around the kitchen table, noting what

it already held with quiet confidence. Joan reappeared. She had been into her makeup and her eyes were drawn out grotesquely by eyeliner, while the rouge had gotten out of hand. Was it simply nerves, Cathy wondered, or had she really meant to apply it to the tip of her nose?

Suddenly the dogs went wild, flinging themselves at the front door as though they would break it down. The uproar rose to a hysterical crescendo as the bell rang. "Bruce, I expect," Jim said, grabbing both dogs' collars before he threw open the door. "Come on in, Bruce. They've been fed, and we've been expecting you." He put out his hand to be shaken in what he hoped was a bluff, understanding, fatherly fashion, and Bruce extended his own in what he hoped was a deferential, affectionate sort of way. Cathy was pleased.

Bruce had the slow, confident manner that satisfies nervous dogs and small, shy children. He was tall, with long blond hair, sliced back over a high, aristocratic forehead, which gave him at times a falsely supercilious air. Now his blue eyes shone. He looked clean and scrubbed from head to toe.

He gave Cathy a hug and a brief kiss. "Bruce, I believe. I'm glad it's you," she said.

"Good, I'm glad you're glad."

He moved on. "Mrs. Cooper, hello. How are you? You're looking fine." He took her right hand in both his hands. "It's good to have you back. And Ms. Huntington. Nice to see you again. It's been some time."

"Since last summer. I see you've grown a mustache, Bruce."

"Oh, this." Bruce gave a cough of laughter, smiled generously, and tugged at the straw-colored thatch that shaded his upper lip. "To hide my sins. At least that's the idea."

"I believe there's some beer in the fridge, Bruce, if you care to look," Jim offered.

"No fear, I'll get there," Bruce replied.

They had all crowded into the kitchen, where Bruce pitched into the pie making with enthusiasm. "How's your artwork going, Mrs. Cooper?"

"Well, I just happen to have a few sketches with me," Joan replied, sounding as though she had learned the line by rote.

"Quite a few, I imagine," Jim added.

"Sounds intriguing, Joan. How about a preview to whet our appetites?" Pat's voice was confident, coaxing, hard to resist.

Thus encouraged, Joan vanished, returning presently with a portfolio, which she opened to a pastel-and-crayon picture of red brick buildings. "The view from my window . . . out there," she explained. "Awful, isn't it?"

"No, it's good," Bruce replied. "At least, I like it."

"You shouldn't say that to please me."

"Honestly. I want to say hello to that picture." Bruce held it at arm's length, then set it up for display on the countertop.

"I used to write poetry and leave it around hoping someone might discover and read it. Nobody did." Joan was smiling her sweet, gentle smile, her hands clasped before her to keep them from shaking.

"Before we get water or grease all over those pictures," Jim interjected, "why don't we wait till after dinner and turn the living room into a gallery?"

So with the best of intentions, the show was postponed. Joan was crushed.

"Mom, can I get you something? Do you dare try a small Dubonnet?"

"Cathy, I don't know about that," Pat interrupted. She narrowed her eyes and shook her head.

Feigning holiday gaiety, Cathy ignored the warning. "What do you say, Mom?"

Alcohol was not prescribed for melancholia, far from it, but Joan, grasping at straws, said, "Why not? You only live once."

They all touched glasses. "To the holidays," Jim said, "and having Joan home."

"To smooth seas and fair breezes," offered Bruce.

"Dad, did you hear? Bruce is being considered for the crew of an ocean race," Cathy said. "A really major race."

"Around the world, actually," Bruce told them. "It'd be quite an honor."

"What about college?" asked Jim.

"I expect it would mean putting off spring term, sir," Bruce admitted. Jim rolled his eyes. "But what a once-in-a-lifetime. . . ." Since childhood Bruce had been in love with boats, planned to major in marine architecture, and hoped one day to design and build his own boats for a charter business in Florida or the West Indies.

"I'd like to ask you something, Bruce," Jim said, his voice, as often, holding an air of accusation.

"Shoot."

"Won't all this sailboat building and charter company take a lot of money?"

"You're not kidding." Bruce laughed.

"And considerable risk, too?"

"Oh, absolutely, sir. The old man won't invest fifty bucks in such a hairbrained scheme. That's a direct quote."

"I can't blame your father, Bruce."

"Gosh, neither do I," Bruce agreed cheerfully.

Jim searched for motive in the young man's face and saw nothing but friendly confidence. "The thing is, sir, I'm in no rush. I've got all the time in the world." Bruce smiled, then laughed again. That was one nice thing about him. He laughed a good deal, yet it was not tiresome. "You should hear the old man when I go on like this. It turns him into Poor Richard. You know, a stitch in time, a penny saved."

At this point Pat and Cathy declared the turkey done to perfection. With ceremony they bore it to the dining room and the old Philadelphia sideboard, a furnishing distinguished in Cooper annals for having contained, on ice until the spring thaw allowed it to go underground, the corpse of a newborn Cooper child, first name long forgotten.

"I hope you're hungry, Joan," Jim urged his wife as Bruce and Cathy carried in the rest of the dinner. "What do they feed you out there these days?"

"Mostly a diet of surprises," Joan said. "One woman ate birdseed. They said it perforated her intestines. She didn't come back. Now the nurses keep the canary cage locked in the office."

No one seemed to know how to comment on this, so there was silence as Jim carved. The turkey fell away in thin white slabs. The gravy was nearly too thick to pour. Pies steamed on the sideboard.

"I think we did all right," Pat observed to Cathy, breaking the silence.

"I'm making a pig of myself," Bruce said. "Hope nobody minds."

Jim heaped up cloudy masses of home-mashed potatoes, flooded them with gravy. "Too much," Cathy said. "That's for Mom, not me."

41

Joan tentatively pushed the food around on her plate, scarcely eating.

"Well," Pat said, "I've got some news. Good news. They've invited me to sing again at La Scala." She smiled broadly over her fork.

"That's wonderful," Jim said. "When?"

"I leave this weekend. I didn't want to let the cat out of the bag until I was absolutely sure. I'll be in Milan for about three weeks. Oh, not performing that long, that's counting rehearsals. But if I get good reviews it should lead to other invitations. So keep your fingers crossed."

Jim was torn. He wished Pat well but sensed he would miss her, perhaps lose entirely the support he had come to count on. With a pang of guilt he said, "With all that nuclear mess over there, is it really a good idea just now?" He didn't have to hear Pat's answer.

She simply shrugged. "That's life on a cannibal isle. Can't let it scare you to death." She put down her fork, crossed her arms firmly, and with her chin down glanced at Jim from under her brows. "Besides, if I hang around here, I may be eaten by your dogs." At forty-one Pat was a flirt, in the way small children are flirts—flirting with life, its experiences, people of either sex, any age: but where her singing voice was concerned, she was driven. If, like her sister, she had made a career in medicine, Pat would not have been content to be a general practitioner. She would have been, or tried to be, a neurosurgeon. Coming from an obscure suburb in Oklahoma without connections or money, it had been like wrestling inside with another person stronger than herself who dragged her where she did not wish or have the strength to go, a stranger with fixed imperatives who directed her life. And so, fallout or no fallout, she was flying to Milan on Sunday night.

"You're sure you're not letting pride run away with you?" Jim asked.

"Never mind about pride, it's my last chance. Jim, all of you, can't you be excited for me? I'm excited. Please?"

"I think it's outstanding," Bruce said, rocking forward in his chair.

"To La Scala," Cathy offered, raising her water glass. The others followed suit.

"We're lucky to have an opera star here at our table," Jim said. "I hope she'll honor us at Christmas, too."

"If you don't, Pat, it's back to the micro and Lean Cuisine," added Cathy.

"Enough about me," Pat said firmly. "We have apple pie, mince pie, pumpkin pie. Should we take dessert into the living room while we have the art show?"

Joan was still trying to eat. For a moment she stopped chewing, then fatalistically began again, her eyes cast down. Apart from the rhythm of her jaws she might have been unconscious. She seemed scarcely able to swallow. Finally a small distention passed down her throat. She took a deep breath and said, "I hope you aren't waiting for me."

"I'm going to put some more wood on the fire," Jim said, rising and pushing in his chair. "Then on with the pies and the art show."

At this Joan sat up still and straight. Her eyes behind the tinted glasses were sad and somewhat frightened. "Listen to the wind," she said. "It must be going to rain. They'll be giving out extra doses of Thorazine to keep us all quiet." She laughed, and it was enough to break Jim's heart. However much he had grown away from Joan, he would always be summoned by her laughter, which was so close to tears.

Cathy looked down at her plate, took a deep breath, and stood up. She could not look at her parents but began clearing the table. Pat and Bruce gave her a hand while Jim put more logs on the fire and Joan began tentatively laying out pictures, insisting that no one really wanted to be bothered.

Bruce took a small sketch, again held it out at arm's length and studied it, set it on a chair, stood back. It didn't seem to be playacting. "So you did this, Mrs. Cooper?" She nodded, as though caught red-handed. "Without a bit of training?" Another nod. "Then I can see why you love it. I really like it. I'm not sure why, but I like it."

"Why do you?" Joan insisted.

"I think it's because it seems so honest. So true. You get the best colors and let them do the work."

"You mean that?" Joan asked, and Bruce returned a clear-eyed, friendly smile that seemed to say, "Don't let me scare you. I'm no threat."

"Then you keep it," continued Joan. "Keep it for me, please?" which Cathy found somehow depressing.

By now the fire had taken hold, bathing the room in golden light. Over the mantle hung the portrait of old Judge Aberdeen Cooper, dark and smoky. The eyes had an accusing stare that, with their quality of following a person about the room, had given Cathy nightmares as a child until she had succeeded in lodging an arrow, the rubber tip removed, right in the middle of the Judge's forehead. On the mantle itself stood a fading daguerreotype of Alexander Cooper in his Civil War uniform, taken a year before he was wounded at Fair Oaks and mustered out. In the corner, emitting a purple glow of dark mahogany, stood the grand piano with sheet music where Joan had dutifully practiced a decade before. Cathy had adamantly refused music lessons, but Bruce could play by ear, and whenever

44

he passed the piano he struck a few random chords, plinkety plunk. The room's overall impact was of fine quality but with an air of neglect. There was no sparkle to the brass sconces. Some of the leather-bound books had begun to flake.

"Now what's this here in the picture, Mom?" Cathy asked, trying to show enthusiasm.

"That's the house roof."

"Is our roof orange?"

"Why, no, but . . ."

"You seem to have painted it orange."

Joan laughed anxiously. "Well, you see, that's the way I felt it. I like to paint things the way they feel to me, not necessarily the way they are."

"Actually," Jim said, "this roof was a kind of orange when I was a kid, before they put on the fireproof shingles."

"You ought to go back to orange, sir," Bruce observed. He held this picture up as well and Joan gazed at it with the fondness of a mother for a child she suspects is ugly and always will be but who is nevertheless beautiful to her.

"It's not really very good," she said. "None of my things are, but painting seems to be the only way I can reach out and touch the world. They seem to say I exist. Do you know what I mean?"

"I guess so, Mom," Cathy replied tentatively.

Joan's hands and eyes were restless as she tried to explain. "Take Renoir," she said. "Even when he was so old and arthritic that the brush had to be tied to his hand, he went on painting. All those sunny puffball clouds radiating light, you know, as if he didn't hurt at all. As though he wasn't just about to die."

Jim stood up, poked at the fire. "If you came home, Joan, I mean more or less permanently, and did some serious oils, maybe I could arrange a show down at the public library. They get some top artists there."

As Cathy knew, this was a worn-out record. In the attic were boxes full of sketches and paintings accumulated from one institution after another, and none of it really good as far as she could judge.

"When I was in France," her mother said, "I painted in oils all the time." With a laugh that was nearly a sob she stepped like Alice easily through the mirror of time into the wonderland of what had been. "We used to bicycle out with cheese and wine and I'd paint the little towns along the Loire. You remember, Pat. What a gentle, lazy river. People there walk more slowly, speak more softly. They take time to talk, I mean really talk; things you'd never mention here."

"And now they have radiation," Jim observed sadly. He had the impression that the French, Parisians at least, were rude to American tourists.

"I loved it in France," Joan went on. "It's still part of me, the best part." To Jim she seemed clad in the soft chrysalis of a dream. "Do you feel that way at all, Pat?" The two had spent their junior year of college studying in France.

"You know that old cartoon in *Punch*," answered Pat, "where the polite but honest curate is asked by his archbishop if he's enjoyed his breakfast egg?" She paused for a response, but none came. "Well, the poor young curate answered, 'Parts of it, Your Grace, were excellent.' When I was twenty, France was definitely a curate's egg. Right now I'm looking forward to Italy, even in the winter."

"Student days. That's all once-upon-a-time except for Cathy and Bruce. Enjoy, kids, while you have the chance," Jim said, putting a log on the fire. Raindrops had begun to course down the black windows. "Pretty soon, it'll just seem like a dream."

"Sometimes," Joan pleaded, "I think we become what we dream. And speaking of dreams, I'm exhausted. So much excitement." She rose, seemed to lose her balance, regained it.

"Are you all right?" Jim asked.

"Just tired."

"You're sure, Mom?" Cathy asked, and with a gesture of unusual concern lightly brushed Joan's forehead with a napkin.

Surprised, Joan touched her brow. It was beaded with sweat, as was her upper lip. "How awful," she whispered. "All that rich food. It's given me a stomach cramp."

Jim put an arm around her. If he had not, she might have collapsed. "Time for this good girl to hit the sack," he said.

"Tub first," Joan replied. "I'm going to soak in water right up to here," she touched a flattened palm to her chin, "without any nurses yanking me out." She laughed sharply. The blood had rushed to her cheeks, and she turned away in confusion. Cathy put her arm around Joan's other side, and with a murmuring of good-nights they helped her up the stairs.

Pills were next. Jim counted out an assortment of colors and shapes, which Joan swallowed with more alacrity than she had the food at the table. Cathy watched in horror.

"There," Jim said. "Now you ought to do just fine."

"I will," Joan agreed. "And Cath, I know it worries you, afraid of becoming like me, gobbling pills."

"Don't be crazy, Mom," Cathy blurted out before she could edit the words.

"But I am, most of the time. I think I always will be. That's why your father ought to get a divorce."

"Now that is crazy, Joan," Jim protested.

"You ought to marry Pat."

"That'll be the day. Pat? She's a loner, on her way to Europe, Lord knows for how long. She'll come back radiated." He tried to joke, but his wife had plugged into his thoughts with the deftness of a switchboard operator.

"She'd marry you if you were free, Jim. She's a beautiful woman, and a good one."

"Not as pretty as you."

"That's right, Mom." Cathy came in for emphasis. It had once been true, but the hospital years had left their mark upon her face as though with lightning, "Mom, would you like a hand getting into the tub?"

"Oh, no, I'm fine. Cramp's gone."

"Then why are you crying? Mom?"

Cathy was tempted to leave it at that but then touched her forefinger to her mother's cheek and felt moisture there like sap flowing from a stricken tree.

"Mom, why so sad? We've had a nice time."

"Because it's so lovely here, and I feel like a vagabond looking through the window and having to move on."

"But that isn't so, Joan," Jim insisted. "You know that."

"You're right. You're both right. That tub will fix me up." Joan smiled gallantly.

"I bought you some Badedas, Mom," Cathy told her.

"No more sulphur soap!" Joan cheered. "The first person to hurry me out of here will be shot at dawn." She had always luxuriated in hot water like a lizard in the sun.

So they let her go, with a small kiss on the cheek from Cathy, cold as an obituary. Joan closed the door, stood alone before the sink and took several slow deep breaths. The eyes that looked back at her from the mirrored medicine cabinet had a look of bewilderment and fear. She slowly looked around the once-familiar bathroom, noticed that someone—Jim? Pat?—had bought new towels. She didn't like the color, but she felt no resentment. Joan turned on the tub faucets. The water at first ran rusty and as cold as the rain on the window.

Leaving her mother alone, going downstairs, made Cathy feel ill at ease. "She needs to be trusted, Cat, given responsibility," Jim said. But even before his wife had become seriously disturbed he could recall listening in the dark to pills plunking into a glass, silently counting to make sure Joan did not take too many. And what if he had dropped off and not heard? That was when he had reluctantly taken custody of her medicines.

By now Pat and Bruce had the dishes under control. Bruce was examining Joan's drawings, but Pat awaited them at the foot of the stairs, where she said out of the blue, "Cathy, you've always seemed an intelligent person to me . . ."

"How would you know that?" Cathy interrupted.

"I assume so, considering the genes. But to practically force liquor on your mother under the circumstances. . . ."

"Force liquor?" Cathy protested. "One tiny glass of Dubonnet?"

"That's all she had," Jim said.

"You know how I feel about liquor, Jim," Pat went on. As evidence she displayed a half-empty bottle of Dubonnet. "Cathy can tell you, this was an unopened bottle."

"I only poured one tiny little glass," Cathy countered.

"Which triggered her off."

"I'm sorry," Cathy said, taken aback as much by Pat's adamancy as by what had happened.

"Cath, it's nothing," Jim insisted. "Joan's fine, soaking away to her heart's content. She is, Pat, honestly. Let's not ruin the evening."

Pat frowned at him. "Let's hope we're lucky this time," she said finally. "Honestly, I hate being a nag."

"I'm not much of a connoisseur," Bruce said, looking up from Joan's drawings, "but I do like some of these."

"They all paint their heads off at Brightsides," Jim said. "They even paint the floors. Joan should have been a writer. I always told her so." Poems poured from Joan's brain as naturally and painfully as childbirth. Jim had offered to take the best to a publisher, but Joan had declined. Like children, they were too personal.

Cathy examined a picture of two figures on a park bench, or perhaps on the seat of a subway car. They sat side by side, eyes darkly hooded, the mouths red gashes, a man and a woman. But there was something about the perspective, the rigidity of the bodies that made it seem quite impossible that they could ever communicate or even become aware of each other. Done in pastels, it left bright dust on Cathy's fingers.

"That picture over the mantle," Bruce asked. "I gather it's someone in the family. I mean, there's a resemblance."

"That's Judge Aberdeen Cooper," Jim explained.

"I'm surprised, sir, you never went for a judgeship. I suppose being a defense attorney, protecting inalienable rights is more exciting."

"I'd have given my right arm to be a judge," Jim said. He did not elaborate, and his tone did not invite questions.

Cathy diplomatically made a toast to happy days, and Jim generously proposed, "To La Scala." Then Bruce sat down at the piano and improvised some stormy passages, finally slumping over the keys with a haggard but triumphant look. They all laughed with relief, the tension of the evening broken.

Cathy snapped on the television for the eleven o'clock news. French farmers were still pouring out contaminated milk, German protestors with bobbing placards clustered outside a U.S. air base.

"Is it that late?" Bruce observed. "I'd been thinking we might go see a flick."

Cathy gave a great involuntary yawn that flowered into a laugh as she tried to stifle it. "A movie at this hour? Anyway, Mom's only here for a day or two. You know."

"Over the weekend, then. Okay?"

"Definitely."

Bruce gave her a quick pecking kiss, then stood a moment grasping her hands, and in the glow of their enthusiasm it would have been hard to say which face looked younger.

"I hate to eat and run," Bruce said, "but my folks will be looking for me." At the door he turned while pulling on his raincoat to wish Pat luck. "It sounds great," he said, and then he was gone.

By now the fire had burned low. Jim brought a wire basket of popping corn. They sat there with heavy eyes watching the embers, too weary to bring the evening to a close. It was Cathy who made the first move. "I ought to check on Mom," she said. "I'll be back for hot and buttered."

She climbed the front stairs, her shadow sliding along before her on the panelled wall like a dark stain. Decorating the upper hall were framed pictures, several of Joan's

51

French scenes, Jim graduating from Columbia Law School, photographs of dogs with slightly faded red, gold, and blue ribbons attached. Cathy had meant to check her parents' bedroom first but hesitated when she saw a light still shining under the bathroom door, then noticed water beginning to puddle onto the hall carpet. She tried the knob. No resistance there. Cathy knocked to be polite and received no answer. Joan must have fallen asleep in the tub. She did not want to simply barge in. She herself hated being caught naked by anyone and she knew her mother was equally modest, so she opened the door a chink and in a voice with more the intonation of prayer than summons said, "Mom, are you ready to go to bed now? You'll get all shriveled up." Receiving no response, Cathy finally entered.

Joan was there all right, and if Cathy usually saw things darker than they were, she wanted now to believe less than she saw. The muscles in her thighs began to flutter. Slowly her hands rose to her cheeks as realization grew. The water in the tub was smoky pink. Like a naked fetus, Joan seemed suspended in the pink water of the womb.

For an instant, Cathy leaned there frozen, her hand braced on the sink. The only sound was the rain flinging itself against the windows in a suicidal effort to break the glass. Then Cathy was screaming for the others.

7

▼▼▼

If the Coopers were in for a troubled night, so was Paul Eichhorn. Built like a barrel, his body was still at sixty-seven a twisted mass of power, the muscles of his shoulders hunched forward in a fixed contraction as if momentarily expecting attack. His round, Teutonic face looked brutal in repose, dishonest when it tried to smile, but what really set Eichhorn apart were his scars. His left nostril had been ripped away from the cheek and imperfectly stitched back. There was a jagged white gash on his throat that vanished inside his collar, while his arms when bare looked like a railroad junction. This left a casual observer wondering what ravages his clothing concealed, and they were many.

Once employed by the Army Special Devices Research Center at Sandy Cliffs, he was out of work. He meant to live on at the gatehouse there, a small stone cottage in the Gothic style, now overgrown with vines, until his lease expired at the end of the year. He had nowhere else to go and felt abused by the world.

An aging recluse, Eichhorn sat staring. A naked bulb that dangled from the ceiling threw down a bitter yellow light. He had no television, could not afford the daily delivery of the *Times,* and the battery in his radio was dead. News was always bad and he remained as much as possible in ignorance of world and local events.

His cottage consisted of four rooms. The bare parlor contained his chair and a small table strewn with *National Geographic* and *Life* magazines from the 1930s and '40s. In the kitchen, the sink was piled with dishes, decay, and mouse droppings. There was a two-burner stove heaped with pots and pans, and a small refrigerator, its door slightly ajar. His bathroom contained a complicated maze of oozing copper pipes that accommodated a pull-chain toilet with a wooden seat and no cover and a shower that when turned on let fall a single jet of cold water. The bedroom, curiously, had six bunks built into one wall, but only Eichhorn slept there amid the sad austerity of what resembled a bankrupt opium den.

Paul Eichhorn had one skill, the training of attack dogs, and in this sole regard he excelled. His was a long career, reaching back to 1939. Dog training was the only subject upon which Eichhorn was at all loquacious. If prompted he would sit forward, the fist of his right hand driven into the bowl of the left, and begin. "Would you believe me if I told you that German is the only language attack dogs understand?" He still believed this and, until recently, in his absolute ability as a trainer. But the young man's pride had become arrogance as he grew older, and the arrogance had yielded to contempt. Recently the contempt had turned upon himself.

His military career had begun at Dachau, far to the south

of his native Rostock. He had moved on to Poland where, during the final retreat, he had stepped on a German mine and been left behind in a hospital. When the first Russians arrived, all the German patients on the first two floors had been thrown out of the windows into the snow to make room for Russian wounded. By the time the fierce Siberians had come to the third floor and the amputees just out of surgery, they were satiated. Some even showed remorse. Eichhorn and a few others were spared. He was even eventually fitted with an artificial limb, later modernized at a hospital in the United States, upon which he moved with a curious gliding, limping walk.

His brooding composure was shaken by the unexpected arrival of a sergeant from the Center's security section. "Good evening, Mr. Eichhorn. Sorry to trouble you." The interview began with Eichhorn returning the greeting in his usual manner, that is, with a suspicious stare. "I was sent to find out if you have any information about a hole in the perimeter fence? Toward the northeast corner?" the sergeant explained patiently.

"Are you accusing me of destroying government property?" Eichhorn replied in such a heavy accent that the sergeant could not decide whether the harsh gutterals were simply the insistent residue of a German accent or the result of damage to the vocal chords. He had to ask Eichhorn to repeat himself and then he replied, "Of course I'm not accusing you." Yet Eichhorn stood accused in his own mind, and correctly so.

"I'm only looking for information."

"Then I am sorry, Sergeant. I cannot help you." He had come to attention, the corded muscles in his body tense with ceremony.

It was not the sergeant's job to make psychological judgments, to decide if Eichhorn told the truth or lied. He simply noted down what he had been told while trying to forget that look in Eichhorn's eyes, the smoldering embers of fading fanaticism.

"Would you care for a beer, Sergeant?" Eichhorn offered, not wanting to seem more guilty than he felt. "It is not chilled."

The sergeant declined and left. Eichhorn stood in the vine-shrouded doorway of what he regarded as his private den. Visitors were rare.

Perhaps he had been a fool, doing what he had done, but it was not for spite, even though they had wronged him. Nor was it disgust with the world, though as he saw it the world was going to hell. Now he was out of a job and soon would have no place to live. At least they had given him good references to the animal shelter in Port Monroe. He could work with any animal, even cats, but dogs had been his life and might well be his death.

He had done what he did because he had an almost religious respect for life in any form. God knows he had learned about the fragility of life, the lack of regard in which it can be held. Toward the end of the war at Auschwitz he had seen the gas chambers and the dogs he had loved and trained being turned on the terrified crowds. My God, the dogs he had trained. He still saw those dogs at night. In dreams they came howling back to haunt him. At first he had slept with his hands clenched, waking to find his palms full of blood.

Now after all these years, creatures all the more lethal had come to Sandy Cliffs. He knew that, and the terrible part was that he loved them and was willing to risk his life to turn them back into the loving friends he had known.

With little formal education, Eichhorn had only suspicion for science and its practitioners. Certainly the program at the Special Devices Research Center was a confirming example. Something had gone terribly wrong with those lovely pups. At first they had stayed with him, eight fine pups rampaging around his cottage, the happiest time Eichhorn could remember. Smiling to himself, he remembered the excursions outside the wire, the old abandoned farmhouse to which he had led them, becoming for a time their leader and they his faithful bonded pack, his only family since the Rostock apartment containing his parents and younger sister had disintegrated in an air raid. But finally the effects of the laboratory tampering began to take over: genetic manipulation, chemical experimentation, all beyond his comprehension. Increasingly the young dogs were withdrawn from his loving care for undisclosed treatments, leaving Eichhorn with the one conviction he refused to abandon, that what they were doing was criminal, as criminal as what had gone on in the dark laboratories of Germany during the war.

To help himself toward sleep, Eichhorn poured a stiff jolt of cheap vodka. All his spare cash went for vodka, for he saw his own primary contribution to the world as self-destruction, but as slowly and comfortably as his sparse funds allowed.

Stretched out on one of the lower bunks, he drowsed. Rain lashed intermittently on the roof. He remembered the incessant rain in Poland. Finally his labored breaths came further and further apart. He was sleeping except for an occasional deep shudder. In sleep he dreamed of wolves, a savage pack that hunted him. Not real wolves, but far vaster creatures out of a Russian fairy tale. They were all teeth and red coiling tongues, terrifying, and yet for each one Eichhorn had a name.

8

On the Saturday afternoon following Thanksgiving the Coopers drove Pat Huntington to the train station in Port Monroe. They drove silently, exhausted in body and spirit. At the school bus stop on Glendale Road Cathy noticed a small, slender girl with a long fall of maple syrup hair standing straight as a young cadet. It was the posture that brought the name to mind: Cindy Lawson. Cathy waved too late, saying, "She didn't see me. We went to grade school together." Cindy was dressed in a cheerleader uniform, probably on her way to the last game of the season. She and Cathy might have been friends if Cathy hadn't been sent away to school.

A cool front bringing rain was expected, but the sun still sparkled on the last few leaves. A blue jay perched on a branch above her tilted his head down and whistled two or three scolding notes. Cindy Lawson prayed that the bus would not be late and that the weather would hold so that her boyfriend, the Monroe High halfback, would have a good day. The bus seemed overdue, but she had confidence that it would get her to the game on time just as it delivered her to school on time five days a week.

Cindy put a hand to her hair, for the breeze had ruffled it. A pheasant flew from a thicket, cackling an alarm. Its wingbeats were like the sudden pumping of her heart. The woods at her back had not yet been developed. A lot of pheasant still lived in Sandy Cliffs. High overhead a wedge of Canadian geese passed, barking like little dogs. For a moment Cindy soared with them and then she was solidly on the ground again and very much alone with the awareness of something not far off, a sound of . . . she was not quite sure. Why didn't the bus just come before the weather spoiled everything? She stood in cloud shadow now and shivered.

Was that someone breathing, trying to scare her, like obscene callers on the telephone? "Hey, you!" she said, a loud voice for so slight a frame. Cindy had a tough act and usually got away with it. "Come on out!" She picked up a rock. There was someone watching her all right. She thought of last summer's flasher and the Van Rath guy who had killed his parents and for all anyone knew was still hiding in the thickets living on snails and berries.

Cindy clasped the stone in her left hand, turned the big school ring around so the seal formed a hard lump under the fingers of her right hand. "Okay," she taunted, "I know you're in there." She saw something uncertainly through the thickets, like the comic strip game—find six birds and five squirrels in this tree. She gave a puzzled laugh that left her lips slightly ajar. The dry litter cried its alarm. A shape rose, darkly indistinct through the tangle of vines, seeming not so much to approach as to grow, imperceptibly at first and then with a hurtling rush.

Drawn by the terrible magnetism of that scent, without cruelty or ignoble passion, not triumphing but terrified, victim of a training deeper than instinct, it lunged, screaming through jagged teeth. For an instant Cindy stood transfixed, terror nailing her feet to the ground. Then with a voiceless cry she fled, but it was a blundering flight without wings and there was no escape.

The Coopers and Pat had arrived at the Port Monroe station. The train from New York waited, still disgorging a few late weekend visitors. Theatergoers on their way to the city purchased tickets. The bored faces of passengers could be seen through steamy glass like holes in broken ice.

"I have a hard time saying good-bye to you, Pat," Jim said. "Isn't that depressing?"

"I'll send a whole bunch of cards," Pat promised. "Wish me luck again." She hugged Cathy, and Cathy gave her a hug back. The truth was, she had gained considerable respect for Pat over the past two days. "And let me know how my old friend's doing."

Then Pat was aboard, waving. The engine leaped, sending a jolt down the cars. Pat swayed, caught herself, and laughed. The long car windows were suddenly illuminated, and like a string of lighted aquarium tanks they flickered out of sight under the Sprucedale Bridge.

"So many people coming and going that I don't know and never will know," Cathy said a bit wistfully.

"Count your blessings," Jim told her.

It would have surprised them both to know that on an

earlier train that day an old resident of Sandy Cliffs had returned. Except for what the police suspected had been a brief but noteworthy visit the summer before, Jared Van Rath had been living on the streets or in shelters for the homeless in New York City. Now he returned home for good.

"Come on, Cat, let's get on our way," Jim said. "It's been one hell of a Thanksgiving. I'm sorry you had to be in on it. You poor kid."

"Poor Mom," Cathy said. "Pat was super. I wish I'd done a little better, somehow. I wish I'd told Mom I loved her. I wish I'd told her I really liked her pictures. I guess you always understand when it's too late." She knew her father blamed himself, but if they had only coped as well as Pat, it might not have happened.

She didn't remember what they told her later, screaming in the dark hallway, "Mom's dead! Mom's dead! Somebody do something! Mom's dead!"

Jim had arrived in seconds, Pat right behind him. "No, she's not dead," Pat had said, crouching beside the tub. Then Cathy, too, heard her mother's breathing, sharp as a knife sliding in and out of a sandy sheath. Jim locked his arms under Joan's and they eased her out of the tub, slipped, and nearly fell on the wet floor. Though losing more and more blood, Joan seemed to be growing rapidly heavier. It was all they could do to drag her across the tiles.

Once in bed, she lay spread-eagled, unconscious, and pitifully vulnerable. Pat brought tape from the medicine cabinet, used a scarf for a tourniquet. Still the blood oozed out.

"Cathy," Jim said, "get the police." She reached for the extension by the bed and for the first time tapped out 911.

61

She heard Pat saying, "Now it's too tight. Here, let me." Carefully she adjusted the tourniquet while Joan murmured, "I think I'm bleeding."

"Don't worry, that's what I'm here for," Pat told her in a firm reassuring tone.

"Oh, God, what am I doing here?" Joan moaned. It must have been a cruel shock for her to return to a world she had meant to leave forever.

Cathy still stood by the phone, her message delivered. She felt totally helpless in the presence of a mother who wanted to die. "Dad," she said, "the police said it might take half an hour for the ambulance to get here."

"Okay, we'll take her ourselves," Jim said. "Cathy, bring the car to the front door." She was a year away from a learner's permit but had practiced with her father on the beach road. She ran down the stairs to the garage.

When she came in the front door Joan was lying on a blanket on the floor, Pat kneeling beside her and crooning in a rhythmic undertone, "Lie still, Joan. We all love you, you must know that. Everyone here loves you." Still Joan pleaded not to go. She wanted to die peacefully at home and not in a hospital glare among strangers.

The three of them got her blanket-wrapped body into the backseat, and Jim slid behind the wheel. "My fault," he said as he drove, ignoring the lights. At this hour there was little traffic. Pat put her hand on his shoulder. "Don't," she said.

"All my fault," he kept repeating with helpless insistence until Cathy said, "Please, Dad." She felt the guilt was equally hers. That one tiny glass of Dubonnet. Without that, who was to say? She kept expecting Pat to bring it up, but not then, or ever after, did a sharp-edged 'I told you so' pass Pat's lips.

Turning in at the hospital they drove up before a double door marked EMERGENCY. Cathy dashed inside to be confronted by a stout nurse carrying a metal tray. "I have an emergency in my car," Cathy told her. With a look of bitter weariness the nurse replied, "I'm not on emergency."

Another, more energetic nurse appeared. "I have an attempted suicide out there," Cathy repeated, regretting the admission immediately.

"Bring the patient here," the nurse said, "I'll get a doctor."

Terror-stricken, Joan clung to Jim until the nurse returned.

A young woman who introduced herself as Doctor Tarkington cheerfully took down the seemingly endless scroll of Joan's medical history, to which Jim and Pat in turn added, amended, agreed. "Oh, my," said the doctor, when it was all down in black and white. "I am sorry. I'm afraid the police will have to be notified, too."

While this was going on another resident with unshaven chin and in Cathy's opinion bleary eyes, worked tactfully behind a curtain to stop the bleeding. Two nurses in blue, wearing white masks, stood by as a secondary slash was closed with stitches, forming a welted ridge. Noticing Cathy's stricken attention, one of the nurses gave the curtain a pull.

"Your wife's going to need some blood," said Doctor Tarkington. "Could you just sign here for permission?"

Jim hesitated, the pen in his hand. "How reliable are those screenings for AIDS?"

"Jim," Pat interrupted, "I can give her blood, if you're worried. I'm O negative. The universal donor." She laughed.

The tests, the slow decanting took over an hour. Cathy

felt dizzy and exhausted. There had been too much blood, too much emotion. It was after three in the morning when Joan was wheeled away to a private room where she lay silent and staring, shrinking away like a little girl whose best beloved grown-ups had undergone a dream change and become beasts of prey.

Doctor Tarkington came in and sat down on a chair beside the bed. Joan seemed to be tiring. "We'll give her some glucose, Mr. Cooper, and her strength'll come back like magic. Otherwise, well, I'm only a resident. Urology's my specialty, and I couldn't venture to guess where your wife's heading. I don't suppose that says a whole lot about the medical profession."

Through it all Joan lay quietly, suffering herself to be discussed like a piece of broken machinery in a repair shop.

Doctor Tarkington stood up finally, saying, "Now the best thing for you guys to do is get some sleep. Check back in the morning."

"Joan? Joan, sweetheart, you get some sleep now. We'll be back in a few hours," Jim said and kissed his wife on the forehead. Her eyes were closed and stayed closed.

Cathy bent close. "Tomorrow, Mom. Now you sleep." In fact, Joan seemed already asleep. Cathy could not bear to kiss the face that looked so like death, yet so like her own. As they drove away from the hospital she felt a shameful, exhausted sense of relief, but with a feeling, too, of something having been painfully removed.

It was after four when Cathy finally fell asleep and she slept hard, without dreams. Jim woke her at ten, saying he and Pat were about to leave for the hospital.

"Wait, Dad, I want to go, too." Her determination was born of shame, and the knowledge of how all her instincts rebelled against going. When they arrived at St. Jude's, Pat stayed in the car, insisting that this should be a family affair.

Joan was clad in a white hospital gown, and her face was nearly as pale as the fabric.

"How are you, Mom?" Cathy asked. "Can I do anything?"

"Just hold me. It's like touching the dead, isn't it?"

"Don't be ridiculous," Cathy insisted. It was the exact thought that had occurred to her.

"I don't want you blaming yourself, Cath. It isn't your fault, or your father's. It never was. Now the only sensible thing for me to do is to go home."

"That's what we want, too," Cathy said soothingly, with a gloomy vision of history repeating itself.

"That's not what I meant."

Then Cathy understood.

"Joan, you've got to fight this loneliness," Jim intervened. "It's weakening you. You've got to fight against going back to that place."

"Jim, Brightsides is my home. I'm not saying it's right."

"Mom, no place like that is home," Cathy pleaded. Each word was forming a small ghost to haunt her later on.

"It is for me," Joan said, smiling. "I have a nurse there, a Miss McGregor. She's like a mother. I'm used to the place. Everything is so much simpler there, even the jokes. Miss McGregor says the path of duty is swallowing pills. And I agree with her."

To Cathy's surprise the smile remained. Her mother seemed to be cherishing it, like a bit of fire she did not want to go out. She stayed with her mother while Jim went out to talk with several physicians and the police. Joan

65

seemed to fall asleep, and Cathy was staring out of the window into the parking lot when Jim returned.

"Well," he said wearily, "that's over with. I talked with the head of the psychiatric department here and he said it probably was best if she did go back. He called Brightsides. There's an ambulance coming in a while."

When they turned from the window Joan was awake, watching them. "Will you keep my sketches for me?" she said. "And write, both of you?"

"Joan, I'll ride out in the ambulance with you," Jim said. "Pat can drive Cathy home."

Joan shook her head, her eyes closed again. "You don't belong there."

"Mom, you'll be home for Christmas? Like last year?"

"I have a feeling I'll never . . ." The thought trailed off. "Of course," Joan's eyes half opened, "Christmas."

They saw her in the trolley to the door where the ambulance waited. "I'll write," she promised. "Nothing will stop me from writing."

It seemed an odd, listless way of parting after such a traumatic event. A kind of anesthesia seemed to impede all their emotions. Cathy felt a deep ache inside her, but it was not sorrow, and her dry kiss on Joan's cheek expressed an honest fatigue of spirit. The ambulance pulled away. It was over.

Cathy took a deep breath. "I don't think she wants to be cured." Her mother seemed so rational and yet so unmistakably condemned, without either seeking or fleeing from it. "Did you ever have an inkling she'd do that sort of thing, Dad?"

"A lot more than an inkling, Cat. A whole lot more."

"I'd like to know."

66

"Later," he promised. "I need to get my breath."

Cathy took hold of his hand. "I know, Dad. Let's go home."

They were almost at the car when Cathy took a deep, shuddery breath, near tears. "She really is hopeless, isn't she?"

"Nothing's ever hopeless," Jim replied, "not as long as you're still breathing. Cathy, don't use Joan as an excuse to cop out. You've had every advantage."

Later that day Joan's sketches were placed with the others in the attic. Cathy examined the bedroom, closet, dresser. There was nothing left of Joan's. With distaste she approached the bathroom. Not a trace. Pat had already scrubbed out the tub.

9

▼▼▼

"Hey, Dad, where are we going?" Cathy wanted to know.

"South," Jim replied. "Bet you didn't know there used to be a bridle path along here. Then some trolley tracks. You wouldn't believe that." The rails, he presumed, were buried in layers of concrete now. Beneath that would be the fossil crescents left by horseshoes, perhaps farther down bare human footprints, for it had once been an Indian trail.

Their destination was the Cooper law office in Mohegan. Trucks as long as barges buffeted by.

"Why the office?" Cathy demanded.

"So you can refresh your recollection, as we lawyers say. And so we can have that constructive talk without interruption," Jim replied casually, knowing that he was perpetrating a dirty trick and might be taken to task for it. Cathy stared silently through the windshield at scenery consisting of shopping centers, old residential areas, more recent condominiums. Once an area of suburban blight, with antique shops that seemed to contain the casual siftings of garbage dumps and store windows where even the mannequins looked despondent in ill-fitting clothes, the county seat of Mohegan was being taken over by the mirrored glass walls of five-story office complexes. The two-family houses were vanishing, but the American Legion hall still displayed its gray antitank gun. They pulled into the parking lot behind the two-story office building built by Jim's father and uncle after World War Two.

"This place could use some paint," Cathy observed, but she went along dutifully. The janitor kept the building open on Saturday.

The inner door read, "Cooper, Powell, and Calder." Jim used his own key to enter. There had been burglaries in the neighborhood recently, mostly thefts of typewriters and word processors. No one was there. He directed his daughter to the law library, where a long, glass-topped table was surrounded with bookshelves and portraits of Cooper lawyers gone by. Jim took the chair at the head of the table, a vast old leather affair.

"I think you can feel it in here," Jim said hopefully. He most certainly could. Cathy looked nonplussed, so he added, "Family tradition, the dignity of the law well served, kiddo. I'd like that for you."

"For me?" Cathy was on her guard.

"Think of yourself as a judge, Cat."

"You've got to be kidding."

"Kidding, hell. I want you to be the first family Portia. And I want you to want it."

"Me? I can't even stay in prep school."

"I'll be speaking to them, Cat. I'll see you're reinstated,

so long as you play ball with me." And before Cathy could think of what to say, he had the Berkshire Academy on the phone and a formula worked out: books to be sent, a work plan to be arranged. If her efforts and attitude measured up, she could be readmitted after the midyear break. "You get all that?" Jim said as he hung up the telephone. "It doesn't include mooning around and feeling sorry for yourself. Or dreaming about chartering boats in the West Indies, which, I might add, is a business that would be better off being run by an attorney."

"Dad, you keep forgetting I'm still a year ahead in school."

"Good. Keep it that way. I wish I had your self-assurance, Cat. If I did, I'd have sold this practice, taken your mom and sailed around the world. Never come back. And you might never have been born. But I didn't, and you were. And I might add, you have the brains. In this world, you can't count on much. People let you down, but the one thing that never fails is education. I hope I'm not boring you to death, but I honestly feel the world is being ruined by lunatics, and that includes most of our politicians. The only defense is to learn. Learn why things happen, and how they can be made to happen otherwise. I kid you not. This is a tough place, and you can make a difference. If you expect to cope with it, you can't beat the discipline of a legal education." Jim hesitated. "Sorry," he said, "I seem to be running off at the mouth. But Cathy, you're exceptionally gifted. And I don't want you to waste all that intelligence."

"Mom's the gifted one," she said sullenly, "and look where it's gotten her. Dad, let's face it, I'm a dime a dozen."

"You won the literary prize last year, didn't you?"

"So what?" Total indifference.

"Don't you have a thing to say to me, Cat?"

"No, Dad, I don't!"

"Must I begin from the beginning?"

"How long is this going to take?"

"As long as need be," he replied, grim and despairing.

"Are you going to yell at me now?" she asked almost hopefully.

"I'm not going to yell at you at all. I'm speaking loudly only for emphasis." He paused, took a deep breath. "Look, may I ask what you have in mind for the future?"

"Just now I don't give a damn about school."

"That's your problem in a nutshell. You don't give a damn." Jim could never quite make up his mind about Cathy. She seemed so often to have her fingers crossed.

Now she whispered toward the floor, "Dad, I didn't mean that."

"Right. And you probably won't mean it the next time. Cat, you just stubbed your toe on about five generations of Coopers. Berkshire men, Princetonians, Columbia University attorneys. A mighty fine bunch, with the possible exception of yours truly. Well, Cat, you're the last of the line. You know, there was a time when a woman wouldn't have been welcome in those institutions. Consider how lucky you are."

"Oh, sure, Dad." She could not keep the sarcasm out of her voice.

"I'd like to speak quite openly to you. May I?"

"If you don't lecture, Dad."

"No lecture. Just do a good job with the schoolwork when it comes, okay?" Cathy nodded affirmation. "I'll let

71

law school and the rest of it go for now, but oh, how I'd love to see you up there on the wall in judge's robes. I can't tell you how proud I'd be."

"You ought to be up there first," she replied, eager to change the subject.

"Would that I were," he said, "but that's all blood under the bridge. Look, it's getting late. Before we both get angry and say things we'll regret, I hope we have an understanding."

"I said I'd do the work. I'll catch up, Dad. I think I've always kept my word to you. But after that, no promises."

Cathy had no intention of voluntarily returning to Berkshire or any other boarding school. She had never wanted to go in the first place. It had first been suggested by one of Joan's therapists as a way of removing her from an unhealthy home environment. Now she had been away so long she scarcely had any friends, never hung out with a group at the club, seldom gossiped on the phone, which was supposed to be the delight of girls her age. There was only Bruce, really, and she supposed that was another thing Jim objected to: Becoming too attached to one guy when she had scarcely dated anyone else.

"Fair enough, Cat," Jim said, accepting the agreement as far as it went. She was not the old Cat anymore. She had grown as tall as her mother. In repose her face barely caught the similarity between this young woman and the funny little Cat with the uncertain eyes and the mouth that didn't know which way to go.

"I'm sorry, Cathy, after all you've been through, to drag you through the coals. I'm getting to be a nasty-tempered old man."

"You sound cynical, Dad."

"Not really, just a sentimental old pessimist. I'm not sure the years give you better ideas as much as they seem to wear out the old notions." By now the room was filled with storm-gray light. What had become of the sunny autumn day? It began to rain. "You going out with Bruce tonight?"

She shook her head. "He went to some boat show."

"What say we pick up Chinese on the way home?"

"Gorge ourselves on butterfly shrimp? Sounds good to me," she agreed.

They drove home in the rain, which thickened into a drumming downpour. At times the headlights shone clearly through the beaded curtains of water, and then the car would hit patches of fog that clung to the road and they dimmed like the moon when snow is on the way.

"What a smell," Cathy said. "I can't wait to engulf solid food, as they say in the dictionary." They had picked up Chinese food in Port Monroe, more than they could possibly eat.

"You'll have to get Bruce over to help us finish it," Jim said.

On Middle Island Road, as they neared the Sound, the fog thickened. And there, without warning, they hit something. "My God!" Jim exclaimed, slamming on the brakes, imagining a jogger crushed beneath the wheels. The impact had been severe. They both got out and noticed a considerable dent in the right front fender. With horrid anticipation they peered beneath the car. Nothing.

"It felt like something heavy," Cathy said. "I mean, that was no raccoon."

"It ought to be dead or out of commission, screaming in pain, or something." They listened in silence. There was only the melody of the rain. The dark foggy evening kept its secrets and finally they drove on.

Near the corner of Glendale three police cars had converged, their red roof lamps sending signals. "I don't believe it, not again," Cathy said. A police matter would inevitably get back to Jim anyway, as village attorney, so he pulled over.

"What's up, Chief?" he asked Chief Mahoney, a grave, headmasterly man whom Jim had known as a brawling boy when his family were tenant farmers on the Van Rath place. Never tested by the more brutal challenges of his trade, Mahoney wore a bland expression bespeaking a comfortable and steady intake of fresh duck eggs, country cream, and butter. Nevertheless, Jim suspected that behind the officer's stolid physiognomy dwelt deep emotions, very possibly violent ones, yearning to be tested against the wave of urban crime that crested toward the suburbs.

"A nasty mess, Counselor," Chief Mahoney replied in a voice rough and abrasive as sandpaper. "Foul play, if you ask me." Despite the rain the chief held his cap in front of his stomach as if he needed to keep his hands busy. Not far away flashbulbs were popping. The rain hung like beads of glass in their brief glare. "They won't have much to show for their efforts," he said, jerking his head toward the photographers.

"Much of what?" Jim asked.

"Why, the scene of the crime, Counselor. You see, a girl was reported missing. She was supposed to be at the football game, cheerleading. Never showed up."

"Cynthia Lawson," Cathy burst out.

"That's right," Mahoney confirmed, leading them with a flashlight down a strip of brown mud and fallen leaves, the

74

path into the woods. Flashbulbs winked again in the dark. "Tracks," said the chief, swinging his light around. "Sorry, it's all mud now. No, there's one." He pointed out a spot where the rain dimpled into tiny pools, forming a pattern. "With this downpour, won't even have that much left by morning. Would you say that was made by a dog?"

Jim squatted down to look. "Too big." Of course the rain might have spread the print, if it was a print. "At least I hope not. If it is, it's a damned big dog, such as I never heard of."

Cathy recalled the prints she'd seen on the beach not long ago. They'd be gone now, and anyway sand had a way of expanding things, making them seem larger, so all she finally said to Chief Mahoney was, "What about Cindy Lawson and all this?"

"We hope nothing, but we're afraid she may have gotten herself in trouble. You see, well, there is a bit of evidence." The officer fumbled in his raincoat pocket. "I don't think your daughter should see this, Counselor." When Cathy did not move, the chief shrugged. Let her have a screaming nightmare if she couldn't take it. "In here," he said of a small self-sealing plastic bag, now gone opaque with the humidity. Holding it low into the beam of his flashlight, he drew open the seam. Inside was a gold school ring, which in turn surrounded the remains of a slender finger, its long nail carefully painted a bright, metallic pink.

10

▼▼▼

Before they garaged the car Cathy and her father agreed
not to speculate upon the episode in the woods, not to
mention Joan or Pat, school, or the legal profession. Cathy
was shaken. She let the dogs out, watching them apprehensively from the well-lit porch. Something terrible had happened, and she was ashamed of herself that the Chinese
food still smelled good when she took it out of the microwave oven.

Jim came downstairs in an old robe, torn under one armpit, and a pair of battered slippers resembling boats burned
at the waterline, the ones he called his security blankets.
He sat down heavily. "I need to decompress, Cath."

"I don't think I've ever seen you decompress," she said.
"Is it possible?"

"Maybe not," he admitted, "but let's give it a try."

They ate on trays before the fire. "You don't mind if
Bruce comes over later and finishes this food? We got too

much." When Jim did not respond immediately, she added, "Bruce is good for uptight people like you and me."

"You're probably right," Jim agreed, though he was not eager for any intrusion just then.

The two dogs dreamed in the firelight. Judge Cooper frowned down from the mantle, the bonsai trees cast weird shadows. Cathy paused over a sparerib. "I honestly think you have it in for Bruce."

"I like Bruce a lot," Jim insisted. "I always have." It was just that Bruce seemed to champion an attitude Jim had gone to painful lengths to control in himself. "I must admit it bothers me the way he seems to think life is something you can . . . well, live like a holiday."

"Is that so bad?"

"Not if you can get away with it. I just don't think you can, over the long haul." The way things were going, maybe Bruce was right after all. Maybe escape was the best answer, the gypsy life, a tiny boat sailing out of this man-made world, endless weeks of blue skies, blazing summer, the blue-shadowed islands of the unknown. As long as the running was to something, and not away. Troubles, Jim had always been taught, came most often from trying to avoid trouble.

"All right," Cathy agreed, "maybe not a vacation, but something good." She remembered the Culloden Kennels, the last time the Cooper family's life had seemed on the right track. "You have to plan on things going well, Dad," she said, knowing deep down she did not believe in happy endings. "I never realized you were such a pessimist."

"I thought we declared a moratorium on serious talk," he replied. "I can put another log on the fire, gnaw on a sparerib, or give you both barrels between the eyes."

"Both barrels, please."

"You asked me the other day if I knew your mother was suicidal. I said I'd talk about it later, and you let me off the hook. The fact is, she was talking about it even before you were born. At first I thought it was poetic license. In my innocence, I imagined a person's thoughts showed in their face. You know, eyes the mirror of the soul . . . not so. Not with Joan. The kennel was going strong when she had her first electric shock treatment. I see that surprises you. I remember her saying, "If they don't cure me this time, promise you'll put me out of my misery. She even talked about how it would be in a warm tub."

Jim paused, cleared his throat. "One night we were out looking for a Christmas tree. I stopped the car at a railroad crossing. We could hear the train coming. I said something like, 'Let's see who's serious.'" He could remember the moment, his eyes and Joan's locked. Was it all pretense, vanity? "In the end, of course, we just waited till the train went by, and got the tree, and came home. We had you to take care of, Cat." He leaned forward in his chair, staring at the fire. "Thank God for that.

"Later that night, when you were in bed and we were putting up the tree," Jim continued, "Joan insisted on talking. I just wanted to finish the tree and go to bed, forget all about it. She kept saying she wasn't afraid of dying but that she wanted her eyes donated to somebody. I think she said her eyes were the best part of her, that they could go on seeing in someone else. I don't think I took it seriously, even then, and if I did, I just wanted to put it aside, get away from it all.

"Then came the summer you were tucked away in camp. We'd gone to the Hamptons to get things together, and one night Joan suddenly ran into the ocean, in an evening dress. I had to go after her." He remembered catching her shoulders in the surf, dragging her back, feeling grateful, even elated. The next few days had been splendid. "Then we came home, and . . . you never heard about that either, Cat."

"Do I want to hear about it?" She stared at the food congealing on her plate.

"I doubt it, but at this point you probably should. It'll explain a few things. A couple of days later she tried it again, in the garage."

"Suicide?"

He nodded. "Exhaust fumes. She had all the puppies with her. She was afraid there'd be no one to look after them. You see, they were never sold. That's what really happened to Culloden Kennels. Not one of them was sold. They died in the car. I'm sorry, Cathy."

She heard this out in silence. Her eyes flashed and her shoulders hunched, but she made no response. She reminded Jim of a toy that had been wound too tightly and is about to burst into pieces.

"I should have explained this before," he said, "but I was afraid you'd be hurt. You were too young."

"It hurts more this way," she replied, her voice cool and collected, too controlled.

"I know. At least I do now."

"I'd rather be dead than be like her," Cathy said. "I wish we were all dead!" Then she took off, up the stairs two at a time, down the hall. Her door slammed loudly. Jim's concern lessened when he heard the strident beat of her stereo.

"That may be the first sensible thing I've heard all day. How's that for cynicism, guys?" he told the bemused dogs.

79

Relieved, they were instantly upon him, thrusting their dark muzzles into his face. "Down, Rev! Down, Taps!" he admonished them, but he held the pair in mock fury, feeling the broad muscles, the heavy bones, that power that distinguishes Shepherds born of German stock from the less formidable American breed. "I don't suppose anything loves as honestly as a dog," he said aloud. "Makes no sense, you guys loving people so much."

Presently Cathy reappeared. "I'm sorry I messed up this evening," she apologized.

"It was my fault," he said.

"I can see now why you're not all that crazy about my raising dogs, Dad."

"Don't get me wrong, Cat. I love the silly things," he replied and put another log on the fire.

Cathy reheated the food. They began again to relax, managed a laugh over a fortune cookie, but the depths of their gloom remained undisturbed. They sat silently, let the food take over. Then Cathy closed her eyes, stretched out her legs toward the hearth, her head on a level with the arms of the chair. Jim pulled out a copy of *The Hobbit,* that tale of good and evil, magic and wonder, in a land and time that never was, reading aloud as he had done years before. The fire burned low with a smoky, coppery glow. Outside, wind and rain battered the house.

11

▼▼▼

Abruptly, the phone in the hall rang. Jim stopped reading, his lips tightened as they always did when the phone rang unexpectedly. He tried to limit the hours when, as village attorney, he had to be available, and if it was one of those "would you be interested in investing?" calls that came so often in the evening he might well bang the receiver down on the table to give the solicitor a shock.

"It's probably only Bruce," Cathy said, already in motion. "If it's for you, are you out?"

"Yes," Jim said, then, "No, use your own judgment. Tell them I just fell down the cellar stairs and I'm lying there with a broken back."

Cathy had the phone to her ear. There was a moment of silence, then she set the phone down on the table. "It was just Pat," she said. "I told her you were at the bottom of the cellar stairs—"

"What?" He was on his feet.

Having achieved the desired effect, she relented. "It's Mayor Kingston. I told him I'd look for you. He sounds kind of hyper."

"He always does."

"I can tell him you're at the bottom—"

"I'm coming, I'm coming." Jim picked up the phone as though it weighed a ton. "The late James Cooper speaking."

The voice at the other end burst into goggling inconsistency, urging Jim to come to the Village Hall immediately. "You sound even more worried than usual," Jim said. "What's up?" The mayor was usually in a chronic state of hyperventilation.

"Worried?" shouted Mayor Kingston. "The sky's coming down in chunks, Jim, and it's just as likely to fall on your head as mine. What we have on our hands is a senseless, brutal murder."

"Murder!" Jim could not help imitating Kingston's voice because he felt the mayor's panic. "I know they found a finger, but—"

"Finger, hell! They have a whole lot more than that, Jim. Now get down here!" The phone was slammed down, and the line buzzed in Jim's ear.

"Okay," Jim said absently, "I'm coming." He stood quietly a moment as though in a vacuum after being rocked by a gust of black wind. He replaced the receiver carefully and stared for a moment at the wall calendar, a fat woman with ten cigarettes blazing in her mouth. "I know how you feel," he said.

"Did I hear the word murder?" Cathy asked from the kitchen. "Cynthia Lawson?"

"I don't know," Jim replied, exchanging his bathrobe for a heavy Irish fisherman's sweater.

"Going like that?"

"What's wrong with it?"

"Not like you, I guess. So casual," Cathy said, grabbing an umbrella from the hall closet.

"Where do you think you're going, old girl?"

"With you," she replied, full of morbid curiosity. "You wouldn't want me here alone with a nut case on the loose?"

It was pitch dark and drizzling as they arrived at the Village Hall. As they parked beside the mayor's Cadillac and two police cars, a face flared between cupped hands. The small meteor of a match hissed into a puddle as they climbed out. Chief Mahoney stood at the doorway.

"So it is murder," Jim said.

"And a coronary, too, if we're not lucky," the chief replied.

Harry Kingston had taken on the job of mayor for the prestige involved, never contemplating the demanding task it had become. As a young man he had been told he was the spitting image of Napoleon. The years had brought him the emperor's ulcers but little of the glory, and his features had molded themselves into the rubbery red corpulence of a stereotypical Soviet commissar.

As Chief Mahoney opened the door to the conference room, Kingston leapt to his feet. "Jim, where've you been? Don't you appreciate we have a monster running amuck in this community? My God . . ." and then, turning on Cathy, "you shouldn't be here, young lady."

"Should I be home alone with a monster running amuck?"

The mayor frowned, then introduced a pipe-smoking stranger who sat beside him at the conference table. "This is the county medical examiner, Jim . . . Horace Baumgartner."

They shook hands solemnly all around. Cathy fought an inclination to wipe her fingers; his hand had been soft and damp.

"I gather you found a body," Jim said.

Between them, the mayor and Chief Mahoney got it out in bits and pieces, a chain of events that Cathy could see inside her head: the Sound View housing project, deserted on a weekend; a Lieutenant Rosencranz, assigned to inspect the area, taking a supper break in one of the nearly completed houses. Midway through a sardine-and-onion sandwich he had become aware of a stain oozing down a wall. Some worker must have overturned a can of red paint on the floor above.

The lieutenant had gone up to investigate. What he had seen there lay on its side, eyes wide, the entire head turned around as though it were looking over its shoulder. His first reaction had been: If she had done that sooner while she was still alive she might not be doing it now.

Downstairs again, Lieutenant Rosencranz had leaned up against the front doorframe and quietly' lost his sardine sandwich. Recovering himself, he had called in to headquarters, reporting the body of a teenage girl, blond hair, blue eyes, wearing the remains of a cheerleader's uniform.

"My God!" Jim exclaimed. "Has the family been notified?"

"Worse," said Mayor Kingston. "They found out on their own."

"I'd barely gotten to the scene myself," explained Chief Mahoney, "when Mrs. Lawson turned up. Seems their son has a police-band radio. You can imagine she was frantic, demanding to see her baby. I caught her halfway up the stairs. I told her it was better not to go up, that even a cop doesn't want to look at things like that."

84

Cathy remembered Cindy's mother, a small blond much like her daughter, and could imagine her denying what she could not force herself to believe, staring helplessly at the very real world in the steadily falling rain.

Eventually, Mahoney went on, she had been escorted home, a doctor called to sedate her, and the medical examiner had arrived to take photographs, collect evidence, and finally remove the remains of Cindy Lawson in a plastic body bag. Two officers did the job easily, for Cindy had been a slim girl, and there was not that much left of her to carry.

Now the medical examiner pushed a brown manila envelope across the table. "These are the pictures," he said. No one seemed anxious to look.

"You go outside, sweetheart," said Jim, and Cathy was on her feet when Baumgartner said, "Did you know this Lawson girl?"

Cathy nodded.

"Think you could make a positive identification? Mrs. Lawson was so hysterical. . . ."

"Well," said Chief Mahoney and opened the envelope reluctantly, clearly not wanting to look, but squeamishness was not what he was paid for. He passed the Polaroid on to the mayor, over whose face came the sort of spasm that might be induced by a stroke. Then it was Jim's turn, who said, "My God, Cathy! You really shouldn't see this."

By now Cathy held the photograph in both hands to keep it from trembling. The picture had evidently been taken upon arrival at the morgue, for a green plastic body bag had been peeled back, curiously like leaves, with Cindy's face the shocking flower that bloomed there, eyes wide and still bright, dilated in disbelief, outrage and pain at what had been done to her body. "There's not a whole lot left of the poor kid." The coronor seemed to apologize.

"That's Cindy's face," she said, swallowing hard.

"But what sort of devil would do that?" the mayor demanded. "And right here in Sandy Cliffs?"

"They're saying there's a pack of killer stray dogs on the loose," said Mahoney, "but I don't buy that."

"Any decent prints?" Jim asked.

"After that rain?" The chief shrugged.

"A dog's print is hard to mistake," Cathy said, recalling the strange ones she had seen in the dusk of Thanksgiving Day. "Four toes in front, one in back."

"What about a tie-in between the Lerner baby and this business? I mean, suppose the Lerner dog was never involved?"

"I never thought it was," said Mahoney.

"Under the circumstances, what else?" Mayor Kingston asked.

Jim shook his head. "It doesn't seem to add up," he said. "My daughter's the dog expert, actually. What do you think, Cat?"

"Wow, how should I know? I mean, I've heard of pariah dogs in India living off human corpses, but an overfed poodle?"

"I only wish someone had taken time to examine that dog's stomach after it was shot," Jim added.

"It never got back to me," Baumgartner defended himself. "I'd have done that routinely. You seem to know a lot about dogs, Miss Cooper. What can you tell me about the arrangement of their teeth?"

"Let's see . . . up front a dog ought to have four canines—they're the long holding, ripping teeth," she ex-

86

plained. "Then behind them are the premolars, for chewing. The last of them can be pretty long, too. They can rip also. The big molars in the back are for grinding. They're supposed to have forty-two teeth, I think, if they have a full set."

"Apart from the size," the medical examiner mused, "can you get some idea of the kind of dog from its bite?"

"I couldn't. Well, some dogs have a narrow jaw, like a collie. They're supposed to have a special way of slashing and jumping back. Some retrievers, like a golden, have big, wide mouths. I've never heard of one biting, though. Then I guess the real fighting breeds, like the pit bulls, are supposed to be hangers-on. Once they fix their teeth they snap their heads back and forth, to drive the teeth farther in. Of course all dogs will shake their prey, to break its back. But most of this is from books, I mean, I don't know firsthand. I've never been bitten. I've never seen a dog's bite."

"I can't imagine a dog creating a mess like that," Jim said. "Not even a mad dog."

Mayor Kingston, who had been brooding stolidly behind his cigar, rode forward in his chair, exclaiming, "Wait one second! We don't need a rabies scare. That would be a disaster."

"I didn't say rabid, I said mad. A dog's mind can snap. We don't have a monopoly on insanity. But even a raving dog with teeth like a buzz saw wouldn't do that," he said, gesturing toward the photographs.

"Then what in blazes did?"

"I haven't the faintest notion," Jim admitted. "There aren't a whole lot of overgrown carnivores around here."

"Except us," Cathy added.

87

"A maniac cannibal?" Kingston shouted. "An over-weight vampire? Just what we need."

"A kind of Jack the Ripper." Cathy pressed her point.

Mayor Kingston half rose from his chair, about to launch a counter barrage, but Mahoney intervened. "I don't like to say it," he began, "but on the force we've been thinking along those lines. Remember that Van Rath character? There are rumors he's been seen around town, and we had one unconfirmed report he was the flasher last summer."

"I don't buy any of this," said the mayor, but the chief went on, asking Jim, "Counselor, you should know something about Van Rath's war record. I've heard he did some very vicious things to prisoners when he was in Vietnam."

"That's my understanding," Jim admitted, not seeming eager to enlarge on the subject other than to add, "I don't think we can entirely rule him out as a possibility."

For a moment this sank in silently. Then Baumgartner said, "Judging from what I've seen, I'd opt for a wolf pack."

"Wolves don't really do that either," Cathy ventured, "only in stories." Little Red Riding Hood had done the wolf a great injustice over the years. Although a dozen wolves could chomp a deer down, bones and all, in fifteen minutes, there was not a proven case of man-killing on record in North America, and not a wolf running free any nearer than Canada. It didn't make sense.

Still Mahoney said, "From what I saw, I tend to agree with Dr. Baumgartner, except I'm sure there haven't been wolves on the Island in a couple of hundred years."

"Is anyone keeping wild animals around here? Remember that guy who kept the bear cub a few years ago? Or any reports of any animals loose from a zoo?" Jim asked. The chief shook his head.

Cathy raised her hand as though in class, asking, "What about the Special Devices Center? Didn't they have some sort of dog program?"

"Very hush hush," Jim admitted. As a village official he had toured the facilities when they had first opened. Security had become tighter since then, and he was surprised that his daughter had heard that much about it. "But I understand the canine business was closed down a while back."

"Rather under a cloud," said Mayor Kingston. "All sorts of odd rumors, that they were feeding the dogs blood plasma, things like that. What about that, Jim?"

"Sounds unlikely. Even so, how would that turn a normal animal into a savage killer?"

"But could they be trained?" asked Kingston.

"Good God, why?" asked the chief.

"Why napalm? Why poison gas? Why Star Wars?" Jim added. "Because if we're given a weapon, we use it, and if we can make it more deadly, so much the better. It's human nature."

And a pretty crummy trick to pull on man's best friend if it were true, it seemed to Cathy. From reading her mother's books she knew the dog was the first wild creature to cast his lot with man, quickly becoming a hunting companion and fellow warrior. Dogs fought for the Assyrians, Egyptians, Persians, Greeks, and Celts. They were Rome's *canes pugnaces* that, as the Empire decayed, entered the arena to fight. With collars spiked with iron they followed the Crusaders and later still marched with the Kaiser's armies. Thirty thousand dogs had dutifully served the Nazi cause. An Irish wolfhound was on record for pulling down and killing an adult bull. Certain breeds, like the pit bull, had been bred to fight, but training could twist a dog's basic nature only so far.

"Didn't the Russians teach dogs to carry explosives under German tanks in the last war?" asked the chief.

"Something of the sort," Jim recalled, "but I'm not sure if it worked out."

"If a dog can be taught to commit suicide," said Mahoney, "don't you think if it were carefully selected and bred and indoctrinated by experts, well, can't you imagine. . . ."

"All right, all right," said the mayor wearily. "I don't know who'll be there at this ungodly hour, but I'll phone the Special Devices Center."

Cathy and the others heard only the mayor's end of the conversation. "September, you say? Successfully concluded? I see." The officer on duty was not acquainted with the purpose or results of the program. "Well, what about the dogs?" Kingston asked. "What do you mean, you can't tell me? I'm the mayor!" After listening for a few more moments, Mayor Kingston said, "Yes, I understand. Thanks for the information. And I want that in writing!" Angry and puzzled, Kingston put down the phone. "He said they destroyed all the dogs. Sixty of them. Said he'd get his commanding officer to send a report to the police. So, for what it's worth, the Special Devices place seems to have a clean bill of health."

Once again they faced a stalemate. The medical examiner controlled a cough in the silence. "Have you something to say?" the mayor demanded.

"Only to repeat myself," said Baumgartner. "Even before the autopsy, I'd stake my reputation that the body was eaten by an animal or animals."

90

"All right," said the mayor, "what next? If I don't come out with some statement and back it up, we'll have one bunch of people locked in their attics and another racing around with shotguns."

"I won't condone any vigilante stuff," said Mahoney sternly.

"What I'd suggest," Jim said, "is that we send a letter to all residents directing them to strictly control their pets and suggesting they drive their children at all times."

"That isn't going to be easy," interrupted the mayor. "There are a lot of families where both parents work. I wonder if the school bus companies would be willing to do door-to-door pickups of the kids?"

"Or we could arrange car pooling," Jim said wearily. "I'd say something about reporting all stray dogs, or anything out of the ordinary. But that under no circumstances should they take independent action unless they're directly threatened. Agreed?"

"I'll rely on you, Jim, for a draft of that letter, okay?" asked Kingston. Jim nodded. "Anything else?"

"I'll be circulating a description of Van Rath. See that it gets to the county level," said Chief Mahoney.

"Good," replied the mayor. "Is that it, then?" He glared at them all with impotent ferocity to freeze their tongues. "All right, I'm already overdue at the club." He rose, snapped a folded sheaf of papers against his leg impatiently. "So, if you'll excuse me. . . ." He motioned Jim to his side. "Jim, I want you and the chief on top of this. Our community has a fine reputation, and I want it to stay that way."

"Poor old tormented mushroom," the chief said when the door closed. "I hope he lives through this."

"You're assuming we're in for more trouble?" Jim asked.

"Wish I didn't," said Mahoney.

Jim tapped his fingers on the table and said, rather unwillingly, "I'm afraid I've got the same notion. You know, Cath, what it reminds me of is when your Mom and I were in East Africa. I mean, seeing what a pride of lions could do." He rose. "Time to go home."

As they drove, Cathy vaguely remembered hearing of a local family raising a lion cub, but the *Port Monroe News* had reported it had been sent to the Bronx Zoo. A lion loose in the neighborhood made about as much sense as a crocodile.

"You didn't say much about that Van Rath guy, Dad. I mean, wasn't he your client once upon a time?"

"To my everlasting regret," Jim replied. This piqued her curiosity, but Jim did not expand on the past other than to say, "If it isn't Van Rath, and Lord knows I hope it isn't, I suppose it could be a drug addict gone berserk on crack, or, as you said, a lunatic Jack the Ripper."

Despite all the talk of dogs and wolves and lions, as far as Cathy was concerned, the four-leggeds were always so much more predictable than people. Not that there was real evidence either way, it was just a feeling in her bones.

"I think the killer's a human being," she burst out as they neared home. "Or something, well, not quite human."

"Count Dracula? I don't know, Cath. Let's leave that sort of thing to Hollywood and the boob tube." He tried to make a joke of the possibility, but neither of them laughed. As for Cathy, she would happily settle for a conventional vampire, against whom there were prescribed weapons: Stakes, silver bullets, even the rays of the sun, which on that cold, wet November night showed little likelihood of shining down on Sandy Cliffs.

92

The cold rain drummed down, pocking the dark, oily surface of the Sound with countless eyes. On the verge of freezing, it beaded the bare branches of the trees above. This was not the sort of night when most human beings, or animals for that matter, would undertake a change of residence, but it suited Jared Van Rath. For him, it was a private night on which he meant to return secretly, an intent curiously at odds with his hooded Day-Glo yellow poncho, which made him as iridescent as a phantom.

A man who thrived on discomfort, if not outright pain, he carried in a nylon backpack the stark essentials of survival: a week's supply of canned and dehydrated food, a collapsible Sterno stove, two disposable lighters, and a small transistor radio. Last of all, the pack contained a can of bright-yellow spray paint.

The path was unfamiliar and overgrown after ten years, but he used his flashlight sparingly. Never mind that he kept running into things. Brambles raked his arm. Tripped by a vine, he sprawled heavily, the backpack thumping down and taking his wind entirely. For a moment he lay still, listening to the rain. Finally he played the flashlight around, discovered he lay in a patch of withered toadstools, all glistening with the wet. Just beyond was the old barn where his father had beaten him countless times. Its paint was gone, and the plank walls bowed outward, near collapse. He felt suddenly like Rip Van Winkle, but with a memory of ten years in and out of Mexico; ten years running wetbacks and heroin. One summer he'd been robbed and beaten in Baja and tried a sort of random revenge by torching a trailer park near La Paz. The wind had been fitful and trailers were not like boats; they did not burn as well.

Jared Van Rath had always been drawn to things he did not love: his parents, boats, this moribund farm. He had always hated the work and had learned to loathe both his mother and father, hating their cruelty as he had come to thrive upon it. Now where hate had been there was a kind of fear, and this, too, had its appeal. He half expected they might haunt the place, in which case they would surely mark his coming with cold delight.

Van Rath stood before the black looming silhouette of the house where he had been born and raised. "Well," he told it, "I'm back," as though the windows might be listening. "What do you think of that?"

He placed a foot on the first step, then the second, and the wood gave back a plaintive cry. There seemed to be elastic in the porch as he approached the door, which swung wide with a sad outcry. Stepping inside, he held his breath, certain of one thing: he was not alone. As he watched, the dark shadow of the kitchen door moved on its hinge. "Father?" he whispered. "Mother?" The door continued its swing. "So you have been waiting for me all these years." Jared Van Rath was home at last, and a bowie knife was clasped in his right hand.

12

▼▼▼

By the Tuesday following Thanksgiving Cathy had done her best to feel at home. The result was that her bedroom looked as though it had been nervously and inexpertly burgled: Drawers pulled out, clothes piled on the rug, dressing table glittering with an assortment of combs and brushes, plastic and old sterling silver, the last with her grandmother's initials, R.C., Rebecca Case.

Having hung on her doorknob a sign in block letters, PREOCCUPIED, Cathy plied the old silver brush through her hair with resolute fury. Presently she heard the car grinding up the gravel driveway; her father was off to a shouting match at the Village Hall. She shivered and yawned. It was cold. She was ready for a good night's sleep, with the bed getting warmer and warmer. Before turning out the light she responded to a scratching at the door: Taps and Reveille. "Lie down, you guys," she said, letting them enter.

Once in bed the blood bumped in her ears. Her skin felt

hot and dry. At first she lay very still, flat on her back, her arms crossed on her chest as though laid out for burial, willing sleep to take her. This didn't work. She had not slept well since the murder, and when she did drift off she usually dreamed of being hunted by something implacable, indistinct, and mutating, at once a dog or wolf, then half-human, crawling forward on silent paws.

Not even the house itself seemed disposed to slumber. It remained as restless as Cathy herself. The very fabric of the walls and ceilings creaked and stirred like the bones and muscles of a living thing. Only the dogs slept contentedly at the foot of her bed, their paws flung out like crouching lions.

If Cathy could have turned her brain over like an hourglass, the same thoughts would have funneled through. So much energy was wasted wanting to take back things she had said and done, or not said and done, particularly where her mother was concerned: Joan, too scared of life to exist except in that place, and Cathy, too horrified at what was going on to show the love she felt.

Under closed lids Cathy rolled her eyes high. Cindy Lawson was still there, behind her eyes, leading the cheers. "Give us a P, give us an O." Cindy must have been all-important to herself, the dazzling center of the universe. She must have hated to die. She must have screamed and covered her eyes.

When Cathy managed to shake off those visions, others rose to confront her. Old Judge Cooper with his hooded eyes. What was this family obsession with being a judge anyway? At least her father had no cause to complain of her homework. Although the assignments had not yet arrived from Berkshire, she was forging ahead with Shakespeare and had even passed up the chance to sail with Bruce in the winter Frostbiting series. But if she could have her way, she would switch to the local Port Monroe school. Maybe if she and her father saw each other every day, they'd get on better. She didn't feel he knew anything about her anymore. Maybe she could even get Culloden Kennels open again. If they could only go back, change things. She seemed to see the path her mother had taken into the darkness and was afraid that for want of another, she herself might helplessly follow.

Outside the wind boomed, whistled, throbbed, sounding like a living thing. The rays of the moon stole across the floor, causing the dogs to stir and lift their heads, ears cocked, listening, listening. Cathy could see the outlines of their pricked ears and the occasional glint from their eyes, depthless and staring. She knew they were sensing something beyond the windows, beyond the gusts that beat round the house, beyond the wild pack of old that myth said ran down the wind pursuing the souls of the ungodly and driving earthly dogs to madness. She seemed to hear it, too, a howling that was more than the wind's imitation. Cathy rose on her elbow, listening, then sank back, preferring to be trapped in bed than stumbling barefoot around the house. If they wanted her soul, let them have it here, where the blankets were warm.

Cathy thought now of Beth Gelert and her mother reading aloud at bedtime of the ever-faithful hound. "Come, Gelert, come, wert never last, Llewelyn's horn to hear." Surely dogs, at least, were never born bad.

Smiling now, she slid slowly into sleep, and only the dogs remained to hear that summons on the wind. It lingered in the air, more felt than heard, the chord modulating in minor thirds and fifths, hornlike and pure. The dogs listened, ears pricked long after the wavering call had been borne away. Taps first, with Reveille following, rose and left the room. Cathy, smiling still, did not note their departure.

Sleep was at a premium in Sandy Cliffs that Tuesday night. Toadlike, hovering uncomfortably behind his dead cigar, Mayor Kingston left it to the village attorney to deal with the alarmed crowd, and the shrill meeting at Village Hall went on and on.

Sleepless, too, was Paul Eichhorn. Stretched on his bunk, arms beneath his head, he gazed up at the ceiling. All day he had been alone with his spiraling thoughts. "I have now been here since ten o'clock and I have not slept. I don't know what the time is, but it is after midnight and I have not slept at all," he said aloud.

The vodka was nearly gone, and yet this time it did not gain the upper hand. It did not bring the peace that passeth understanding. Eichhorn could feel the doomed world spinning under his bed, and his ears rang with the breakers of a black sea that rolled in and shattered on iron cliffs. "I'm a dog trainer," he assured himself. "The best." He had put the finest dogs alive through their paces.

Clumsily Eichhorn thumbed through a scrapbook that he had drawn from beneath his pillow. He smiled at pictures of puppies. There was even a snapshot taken at the abandoned farm where he and the young dogs had played together, becoming bonded. They were what he regarded as his family, his pack. Other pictures showed the trainer with full-grown animals, massive creatures, their front legs hooked over his shoulders. Just because a couple of foolish assistants had been hurt, it was not fair to blame the animals, precisely when he knew without a doubt the program was on the verge of success. God would forgive him for taking what exception he could to the extermination order, or so he had assumed until now.

He had done what he had to with the fence. Just one more generation! He had given it life—and now! Eichhorn had finally seen the newspapers. A baby dead in its playpen; by itself that meant nothing, but now the cheerleader with her bouncing blond hair, who used to wave at him as she jogged along Middle Island Road. He had come to expect her in late afternoon, to be there to receive her remote friendship. While he was waiting for her, the Van Rath boy had come slinking down the road with a backpack. Eichhorn had recognized him, though he looked older now, and as he watched he saw Van Rath twice glance over his shoulder as though pursued. He's like my babies, Eichhorn thought, outcast and hunted.

Eichhorn steadily drained the last of the vodka. The old wall clock from Germany whirred as though it had something lodged in its throat. Gears struggled to record the hour and subsided after two rapid, metallic hiccups. "I'm coming apart bit by bit," Eichhorn told himself. "Bit by bit." Promise had vanished from the earth except the promise of worse. Hope had failed; only the cruel and deadly remained. In the dark of the night-bound gatehouse, a plaintive cry rose slowly, like a vine growing in the blackness. It could have been the howling of a dog in pain, but the sound issued from the lips of the sleepless man.

13

▼▼▼

A week later, as a reward for conscientious study and because Christmas was hurtling upon them, like it or not, Jim took his daughter shopping: City shops in a suburban setting, then the lumberyard as a last stop. Jim wanted to repair the old dog pen and kennel enclosure because of the growing hysteria. The car radio summed it up.

"Sandy Cliffs, once the playground of millionaire sportsmen and until recently a quiet, posh Long Island suburb, has recently been the scene of two brutal and mysterious murders. Ten-month-old Randall Lerner was killed in his playpen by an unknown assailant, and last week seventeen-year-old Cynthia Lawson was gruesomely slain. Local and county police suspect a large dog or other animal. Dozens of local pets have been poisoned, and today a Doberman pinscher was fatally shot by an unknown marksman while alone in its owner's Mercedes."

As both Jim and Cathy knew, this was only the surface.

By some insane coincidence or design, rage had spilled over to the village cat population, a number of which had turned up with amputated tails.

For the moment the Coopers were full of commercial Christmas cheer: Crowds, canned carols. "I guess I'm glad it's only once a year," Jim remarked as they pulled up before the front door.

"There's the phone." By the time Cathy had unlocked the door and picked up the receiver, it was silent. "Probably just a burglar casing the joint."

Sandy Cliffs shared with most other opulent suburban communities the paranoia of modern living. Over half the homes had burglar alarms hooked up to the police station. The Coopers had always relied on their dogs. "I can remember when we never thought twice about leaving the door unlocked," said Jim.

"There it goes again," Cathy interrupted. "Cooper residence," she said into the cold black ear. "It's a Dr. Simon for you, Dad."

Jim sighed and took the phone, saying, "Yes," and "Yes," again, with his expression changing in one sharp exhalation. In a moment he turned to Cathy and said in a flat voice, "Joan's dead."

"Dead?" repeated Cathy, a hollow echo. She sat down suddenly, feeling as though she'd received a blow. Dead! There were times, perhaps, when she had almost secretly wished it, wished for a resolution of any sort. Times when she had dreaded it or imagined it, but not like this, not from a stranger over the phone. Her mother had killed herself among strangers. She felt dazed, her mind a blank.

Jim was a long time listening. Finally he replaced the phone in its cradle. "Oh, Cath," he said, "she died, and I wasn't even there." For the first time Cathy could recall since her childhood, her father spontaneously put his arms around her. She knew he was silently crying, felt the shudders run through his body. He released her and she saw his face, distorted with grief. Tears flowed all the way to his chin. She had never seen him display so much emotion; it was like seeing sculpture weep.

Cathy could not cry, not yet. A taut rope had begun to twist itself in her stomach and formed more and more kinks.

"I assumed it was suicide," Jim said, wiping his eyes.

"Then we killed her!" Cathy shot back, her face contorted by the ugliness of self-accusation. "We killed her!"

Jim stared, feeling her guilt as well as his own, a mutual repulsion that formed an intense bond. He shook his head. "Dr. Simon said it wasn't suicide. She just keeled over."

"And?" Cathy urged. She had to hear it all, sensing that no matter how it added up, the sum was murder.

"An attendant found her when she didn't come to breakfast. She'd gone to the bathroom. It must have been all those drugs over the years. Maybe her heart simply gave out."

Cathy could see her mother peering from behind her door into the endless freezing corridor, going on tiptoe, thin arms clasping her thin body, then dying alone without a cry, inscrutable, unprotesting, upon the gray cement floor, the loneliest death of all.

"The doctor said it was as if she'd fallen asleep, with one hand under her cheek." Like a child, Jim thought, an aging, sad, thin, lonely child lying alone on that cold floor.

He took a deep, uneven breath. "Of course there'll be an autopsy. . . . No, Cat," he countered her protest, "it's the law." But the autopsy could only give a medical name to death by fear and despair, death because there was nowhere else to go. "I passed on that 'eyes to science' request your mom wanted. And cremation. Is that okay, Cathy?"

"Sure," she acquiesced numbly. The thought of an open casket or even a funeral made her feel sick. Her real questions lingered. Did we kill her? Did I? Oh, Mom!

There was the rest of the day to stumble through, phone calls to be made. Jim absently watered the bonsai trees, a splash here, a splash there, most of it puddling on the windowsill. Why am I doing this? he asked himself. Just to be doing something? It had been so long since Joan had been factored into the day-to-day routine, and yet suddenly there was a new vacuum in their lives. It was really not Joan that was missing, he realized, but hope. Hope had been living in the house long after she had left.

Cathy stared out of the window. She took a shuddering breath near tears. Jim came into the living room, lit the fire, made himself a drink. "Want something, Cat? You're not too young at a time like this."

She shook her head. They sat before the fire, watching it burn down to a pulsing glow. "It's funny," she said finally, "in a way. I mean, Mom's been dead for years."

"I was just thinking, Cat, about when your mom came back from her junior year abroad. She wasn't all that much older than you are now. Her parents met her plane, and I didn't see her till the next day. It was June, and she was walking down the beach straight for me."

"Oh, Jim, France! France! What'll I do? I'm bursting with it," Joan had said. Then there had been all the pictures he had inspected dutifully, wondering why anyone went to such trouble to make nasty messes. It hardly mattered, for they were falling in love, and they'd have an attic large enough to store any number of paintings.

Four years later had come the best time of all, East Africa. "I wish you could have been there, Cat. You missed out by nine months or so." Paradise, the way the world used to be, young and carefree and marvelously beautiful, without drabness or sorrow or boredom. "The old buffaloes in the morning mist at Ngorongoro," Jim recalled. He saw again the dark lip of the crater seeming to pour down waterfalls of cloud into the lake at the bottom, rimmed pink with flamingoes. "I don't know if there are any rhinos left now, even there."

He remembered Joan's brief foray into running an art gallery. "Almost ruined me." And then the kennel, ". . . just as bad." Yet he smiled, remembering good times.

"I wonder, I mean . . . if it's because of me?" Cathy interjected her own concerns.

"Come again, Cat?"

"I mean, just having me. You know, pregnancy. That postpartum stuff. Maybe biologically I made it go wrong for her."

It was true that not long after Cathy's birth Joan had begun complaining aloud to herself, swearing at the vacuum cleaner or the United Nations, belaboring the broom and the Long Island Lighting Company, damning her wedding china, admonishing the silverware and the afternoon game shows.

"I wish you could have seen us in those early days," Jim insisted.

"Before me."

"No, no, just before things began to slide. I'm sure I'm

104

the one at fault, not you, Cath. Honestly, I just don't know. . . ." His voice trailed off, for in looking at his daughter Jim was driven to the conclusion that suddenly her youth was over. Cathy's chin moved in small affirmative nods as though she could not trust herself to speak or even look at her father. She was biting her lower lip. By now both had tears in their eyes. "Well, I'm glad to see you still remember how it's done," Jim said.

"It's just that, sometimes, it seems that maybe Mom was right. I mean, what's the point?"

"Uh–uh, Cat," Jim told her. "None of that. I don't know. I guess with me, life itself comes as close as anything to being the point. I haven't a clue what we're supposed to do with it. Sometimes I pretend to, as you well know, but I don't, really. It's all we've got, and if something terrible happens, like now, and you think the world ought to stop . . . well, it doesn't. Not yet, anyway. People keep muddling through. The world keeps jogging along, not because it matters, but because it doesn't. And, Cath, even when everything seems to be going to hell and you wish you were dead and you go to bed with a whopping drink hoping maybe you won't wake up, you hang on, because something beautiful is about to happen."

"What, Daddy?" she asked in a small, choked voice. Oh, God, thought Jim, she hasn't called me Daddy for years and years.

"The dawn, Cat. You can count on it. Another day. All it takes is the teeth to hang on with. You've got 'em, Cat, I know you have."

14

▼▼▼

After a sleepless night Paul Eichhorn clung to his bunk throughout the morning hours. His head felt full of broken glass, and a hiccup left a nasty taste of bile in his mouth. Finally he rose and showered, stared at himself in the mirror. He was a vision of matted hair, which stood up on his head like a dipped rooster's. His eyes were bloodshot pebbles, not fiery, but cold as the recollection of family death.

What had gone wrong? It was not his doing. It never had been. He had only trained the dogs. They had messed it up in the lab, as usual, with their gene splicing, playing God with eugenics. They should have asked him before they started in on their oversized mice and then, if you could do it with mice, why not with dogs? He had known Doctor Mengele in the old days well enough to say, "Good day, Herr Doktor." Later, Eichhorn had heard about Mengele's revolting experiments with midgets and twins. They should have asked him his opinion, the bright boys in the lab, but of course they never did.

Before long they would blow everything up. That did not really bother Eichhorn, for what was a billion years of evolution worth if poised on the work of a scientist whose curiosity extended beyond his wisdom, on the failure of a computer chip, or on the zeal of a fanatic? What did it matter if the human race vanished? Who would be left to mourn it? Eichhorn told himself this again and again, yet he must have cared enough to get drunk and oblivious night after night.

His first mistake had been looking the other way, just as he had ignored the mounting horror of Auschwitz, so that what was unacceptable one day, became commonplace the next. To keep his family alive in Rostock, that had been his excuse then, until their peril was ended by a British bomber. Recently it had been his need to keep his dog family alive, one step at a time, and the chance he could undo the machinations of science. He had never reckoned further, had blotted out the possibilities. Now, if it weren't that lunatic Van Rath, what else could be responsible? Perhaps he'd had a chance to prevent what was now being called the Sandy Cliffs Horror before it started. But that was hindsight. Now there was no one else who understood and might end it with some shred of decency, before Sandy Cliffs exterminated all its dogs in a mania of vindictiveness.

It was three o'clock that afternoon when Eichhorn took his first drink, not to get drunk, but to bolster his resolve. He pulled out his old leather jackboots. Funny, how they had survived and one of his legs had not. Then came the heavily padded canvas armor he had worn during the training sessions. Striving to jerk it on, Eichhorn for an instant became engulfed in the rigid garment. He staggered, regained control. Next he tested the flashlight. Good. The ancient cigarette lighter with the twisted cross upon it worked as always. The padded gauntlets he gripped beneath his left armpit.

From a cupboard he pulled down a red plastic two-gallon can of gasoline. No, no need for that, not yet. He chose a stout fire ax instead. Over his large, gnarled hands, now damp with sweat, he slowly pulled on the stiff gauntlets.

Thus clad and armed, Eichhorn briefly imagined himself a knight errant, Siegfried, a way he had not felt in over forty years. He saw an image of evil boiling up in the world like an irresistible tide to drown humanity, and only he could do battle and win or die.

When Paul Eichhorn went forth into the dusk he walked like machinery, his hands out from his sides as if to ward off interference. He should have clanked. The sky overhead was clear, the first frosty stars appearing. A thin shaving of a moon hung over him, clear and pure, and he cursed its faint light. Slowly, heavily, favoring his artificial leg, he trudged into the woods like a primitive being burdened with mankind's first responsibilities. He felt alone in the universe.

15

▼▼▼
▼

The moon that guided Paul Eichhorn's steps through the woods north of the Special Devices Research Center threw down harsh shadows upon the parking lot at the Village Hall. There was a space reserved for the village attorney, and Jim rolled into it, the last one available. "I hate this stuff," he told Cathy, who had come along—out of curiosity, she told Jim, but really because she was afraid to be at home alone.

The threatened fireworks were already in evidence, and a babble of voices told them the public hearing room was already packed. Mayor Kingston intercepted them in the hall, his round face already flushed. "Where the hell have you been, Jim?" he demanded, though the meeting was not scheduled to begin for another ten minutes. Jim tried to calm him but to no avail. "Don't you worry about my blood pressure, Jim. Worry about my sanity. This village is going crazy." The Lawsons had arrived early, their first appearance since their daughter's funeral, and that had every-one stirred up. In the mayor's opinion, if they could not clear this up quickly, the Republican administration, which had governed wisely and well since the village's incorpora-tion, would get itself voted out and the liberals would have a field day.

Although there had been no incident since the death of Cynthia Lawson, there had been no revelations either. Panic fed on ignorance. Both in Sandy Cliffs and Port Monroe people were turning their own dogs over to the police, and the police, hesitant to call the animal warden to destroy the pets, turned to the local animal shelter, which in turn was harassed by anonymous phone calls and a bomb threat. Even more alarmed and self-righteous were the homeowners who had never owned an animal. All those who needed to vent their hysteria seemed to have con-verged on the Village Hall this evening.

The argument centered on supplementing the police with civilian volunteers. Chief Mahoney was absorbing all this with his lips moving silently, as though he were already ar-ranging what he had to say. "Vigilantes? No, I don't think we need that. This isn't Dodge City. Now!" He cast a pen-etrating gaze around the assembly. "Though we don't want a whole lot of innocent pets being put down or abandoned, there's a remote contingency that the perpetrator might be a licensed neighborhood dog. With the present crime rate, a great many fully trained—and some not so well trained—attack dogs have found their way into this community. I assume anyone with such a dog who has the least suspicion it might be a vicious animal will report to me or one of the village officers." The chief paused. "Well, thank you for your attention," he said finally. "Now I think we should

110

hear from someone who's far more expert when it comes to dogs than I am, our village attorney, James Cooper."

Cathy knew very well her father was not prepared for this. At first he rested his fingers on the table that served as a rostrum, smiled mechanically, cleared his throat. The silence grew restless.

"I think what Chief Mahoney means," Jim said, "is that I've raised a lot of dogs. Good dogs. I still have a couple and, serious as the situation is, it has to be kept in perspective. The average dog has adjusted very well to the pressures of modern life; better, for the most part, than we humans have. Believe me, you're far more likely to be murdered by a violent spouse than by anything on four legs around here. I know we all grew up on Little Red Riding Hood, but that's where it should be left, in fairy stories."

At this point Cathy first became aware of Mrs. Lawson, whose face seemed to be dissolving into a mask of ugly red lines. "Oh, how funny. Isn't this funny?" she exclaimed, producing a paroxysm of false laughter, while her husband plucked at her sleeve. With a sob, she turned her head to his shoulder, but if she wept it was silent agony.

"So remember this," Jim struggled on. "Until Chief Mahoney gives us the okay, report any suspicious-looking strays, but don't provoke them. Above all, don't panic and run. A predator is always more apt to attack a victim in flight."

"This is all terribly instructive," Sharon Lawson burst in. "Terribly, terribly instructive, but my little girl was torn to pieces. Why? My God, can't any of you do anything except talk?"

"Mrs. Lawson, I assure you. . . ." Jim pleaded. Cathy sensed he could scarcely even look at the bereaved woman.

"Mr. Cooper, you don't assure me of anything," she shot back before giving way to tears again. Then her husband said, "Pardon us. Please . . . my wife . . . a terrible trial," he apologized while steering her toward the door.

Jim was saying, "You have our pledge." He was the village official personified. "There is nothing to fear. Everything is under control."

He can't mean that, Cathy thought, not possibly. Even then his words seemed calculated to return as small ghosts to haunt all those responsible for village affairs.

With the departure of the Lawsons, others followed, wanting to be at home behind locked doors. The meeting was effectively over.

"Mr. Cooper, this village is in for more trouble," Chief Mahoney predicted, "and what you just said won't help a bit."

"I know it," Jim admitted, looking suddenly exhausted. "That was a damn fool thing to say. I've been . . . perhaps you heard about my wife."

"Yes, I'm sorry, Counselor," Mahoney replied. Embarrassed, he looked at his cap, which he was rotating nervously in both hands. "I expect we ought to tell you, we came up with a knife, a bowie knife, not far from the scene. It's at the lab now, but what with the rain they're not very optimistic."

"You'll let me see the report," Jim said. He only wanted to steer Cathy to the car, but Mayor Kingston now stood in their way, an object to be got round.

Having overheard the exchange, Kingston began, "I can't tell you how distressed I was to hear about Joan."

"She'd been a burden to herself for a long time," Jim said wearily.

112

"You had every reason not to come here at all, Jim. Every reason under the sun," the mayor continued, back now to his own concerns. "But Jim, since you did, why did you have to fix us up like that? You know nothing's under control. I suppose you've heard the police found a vicious-looking knife. Lord help us if that gets out. Next time they'll lynch the lot of us. I haven't slept since that girl was killed, but now that I know 'everything's under control,'" he said sarcastically, "why, I'll sleep like a baby. It's on the record; I have your word on it."

"Go home, Harry. Things'll look better in the morning."

This reassurance was hollow at best. Something still lurked out there, the boogeyman, the hound of hell, Cerberus, the three-headed guardian of the underworld, but neither Cathy nor Jim cared to dwell upon that nightmare any more than they could rehash the might-have-beens where Joan was concerned. Their mourning was becoming a private thing, and they drove home in silence under a black December sky full of stars as cold and sharp as chips of ice.

Finally Cathy said, "Guess Pat gets back next week."

"Last thing I heard was the eighteenth. I'm planning to meet her plane, pick up her mail and all, so she can come right out for the holidays," Jim added.

"Is it okay if I come with you?" Cathy asked, and then, out of the blue, "You ought to marry her."

"What a suggestion, coming from you, Cat," Jim replied, startled. In fact, it had occurred to him long before Joan's last decline, but he had dismissed further speculation with a sense of shame. Jim was old-fashioned. He believed in "until death do us part."

"You know," he said, "Pat doesn't know about Joan."

113

But Cathy persisted. "Honestly, I'm very fond of Pat."

"You didn't used to be, Cath."

"Over Thanksgiving she really . . . well, took charge."

"With Pat, I'm afraid, her career comes first, " Jim said. There hadn't even been one postcard from Milan. That was Pat's sort of faithfulness, not to write, to permit herself to be forgotten. "She didn't have a very nice time back home in Oklahoma. You know how she feels about drinking, and she's not just being evangelical. Her father was a drunk, a nasty one. He gave her a rough time, even tried to molest her. Rather tentatively, I gather, but then drunks tend to fumble. All the same, I can see where it might make a woman hesitant about men."

"Oh, yuck!" Cathy said. "That's disgusting. Poor Pat. What a horrible thing to have happen. But Dad," she turned to Jim, "I think she likes you a lot. I mean, why not?"

"I don't mean to sound suspicious, but Cath, are you trying to butter me up?"

"Not at all. But I was thinking that if I went to school here, we'd be more of a family. I've been away at school so much I don't even have any friends around here anymore."

True, thought Jim. "No more policy decisions tonight," he said. "I've put my foot in my mouth once already. I just want you to be able to get into a good college and a good law school."

"That's a long way off, Dad. And when the time comes," and she did not seriously expect it ever would, "the choice has to be mine."

"When you were born, kiddo, a star stood over our house. You're our next generation, the best of your mom and me, a lot of good material."

114

And a lot of bad, she thought, and shivered. "Sure," she said aloud.

Jim took one hand from the wheel, gave her arm a brief squeeze. "You're sounding like a spiteful mutt, Cath. Don't be hard-boiled. I'm counting on you. That's why I seem to push."

"And if I set my heart on something else?"

"You haven't yet. I mean, I don't think you have. We both need time, if this crazy world is willing to give us any."

16

▼▼▼

While the villagers argued and made promises they could not keep, Paul Eichhorn hurled himself along with harsh thrusts of his one good leg. He had gained the beach where Cathy had walked at Thanksgiving. It was deserted. The tide was on the rise and the profound silence was broken only by the lapping of tiny waves and the drag of pebbles.

Long before he came to the road that Cathy had taken home, Eichhorn laboriously climbed the dune. Even in the dark he knew the narrow path that led through bayberry and sumac, then under the trees standing tall and bare: black walnut and locust. Here the earth was deeply carpeted with the recent fall of leaves. His feet sank into this surface at each step and mud oozed up. From high in the branches the moon glared down on his slow progress like a blind slit eye.

The impression was trancelike until a small creature darted from the shadow into the moon's ghostly path. Startled, Eichhorn whirled the ax that had been loosely grasped in his right hand once around his head and let fly. There was a dull thud, and he reached down to retrieve his weapon. The rabbit had been cleanly cut in half.

Eichhorn progressed with a groping roll, his feet splayed wide as he moved along a split-rail fence overgrown with wild grapevines and blackberry brambles. Where an old cow barn had fallen and the earth was rich with ancient manure, numberless toadstools had pushed up, sprouting fleshy fingers in such spreading profusion that Eichhorn paused. How could this be, in December? He had the odd presentiment of their moving toward him, around him. Had he not read about a cancer-ridden town infested with growth-covered trees?

Shaking off his sense of unease, Eichhorn lurched to the other side of the barn where a pond barred his way, its motionless surface like thick black varnish. The old Van Rath house frowned down upon him, not simply an abandoned house but something more, a presence. He had the awareness of another personality, a mind, old and terrible and aware, waiting and listening for sounds of life outside, waiting as a spider waits, yet waiting in fear. He had been here before, numerous times, but never like this, never at night, never alone.

With less stolid resolve Eichhorn might have turned and fled, leaving it to the bright young men and women in the lab to work things out. Instead he moved toward the sagging porch. A twig snapped underfoot, harsh thunder in his ears.

On the porch there was no way of making his artificial leg behave, and each step rang like a coffin tap. Broken glass ground under his boots and he nearly stumbled over a pile of leather-bound books, rat-gnawed, with broken, flaking spines. Where he came from they burned books nobody wanted. He tried a window spattered with fly husks. It would not budge, but the door though spray-painted with the word BEWARE, was not locked. He eased it open soundlessly. Dry litter whispered underfoot and there was the pungent smell of old wood, old leather, mildewed blankets, and backed drains, the smell of neglect.

"Cold as a barracks," Eichhorn told himself. His flashlight was dimming already; he should never have bought those cheap batteries on sale. But he was prepared. He produced two candle stubs, lit them with his lighter, set one burning candle on a table and with this reference point moved on, holding the other candle.

The ceilings were high, invisibly so. It would have been cold even in summer. He saw only the faint outlines of books etched out in the flickering light. With the candle throwing a small, fluttering halo he moved from room to room, staying close to the walls lest the floorboards cry out. Careful of the piles of newspapers on the stairs. He picked up a Baedecker guide to Spain, 1926, postcards from the same era. The Van Raths had been country gentry once, before subsiding into subsistence farmers.

In what must have been the parlor, thick leaded mirrors stood floor to ceiling, old, brown, and silvery as the surface of the pond, a passageway into a fading past where he was startled to see an ectoplasmic face peering from another time and place, his own but somehow younger. He might have been again in his old home in Rostock, for so he had stood in the ruins just after the war, his young face pale, thin, and troubled, looking back from the remains of a shattered mirror. He shook his head to banish the ghosts.

118

Another mirror lay fractured on the floor, its surface etched with radiating frosty scars. Stones, he guessed, or bullets. There had been bullet scars on the remains of the Rostock building, and as he stood in the dark he half expected to hear Russian voices from the street. He had to remind himself there was no street here and no sound except the soft scurrying of some small animal within the walls.

The candle would not last long. It was so like the dream candle with which as a child he had been sent away from the dinner table, too short to see him all the way to bed or carry him safe back again, long enough only to lose him in the blind corridors of fearful sleep.

The prospect of being caught in the dark, unfamiliar rooms made Eichhorn hesitate. The cellar was the only part of the building he knew, and he had always entered it from the outside stone steps, never through the house. The cellar was where he would have to go eventually, and yet a horrid curiosity about the house, about himself, drew him on. He must hurry if he were to see it all, for if he did not he knew he would have to return. That he did not want to do, any more than he could have endured another visit to the war-gutted streets of Rostock. Keeping a hand on the wall because the stair railing was gone, he climbed to the second floor. With the feeling that someone lay dead on the other side, he gingerly pushed open a door from whose latch dangled a broken chain.

Revealed was a small room chaotically piled with a hodgepodge of Victorian furniture such as a woman without moderation or good taste might accumulate, the domestic treasures that must in time have become the one tangible reality in a world of change and loss. All such me-

mentos had vanished from his parents' home when he had returned. Yet Eichhorn had seen it all before, even to the futile bars on the windows and the ludicrous scythe that hung on the wall, left there by some nightmare lunatic, the last demented survivor of the Van Raths, death's own weary weapon in a final stronghold against the inevitable.

On a dust-covered dressing table beneath the scythe stood a rusty lantern, that still contained a shred of wick and what sounded, when he shook it, like a full supply of kerosene. Lifting the glass chimney, the old soldier transferred a butterfly of flame from the expiring candle. Shadows leapt up in sharp relief. The windows stood out slate black; no trace of moonlight showed through the drawn shutters. Across a stretch of wall some vandal had written in yellow spray paint MOTHER'S ROOM, a legend more eerie than the usual four-letter words.

Outside the furniture-piled room, newspaper-strewn hallways led left and right. Another flight of steep, narrow stairs rose upward and, like that dream-drawn German boy, he followed them, not caring if they led to disaster.

A hinged trapdoor opened upon a vast unfurnished attic filled with large wooden chests that had mostly vomited up their contents: some fine linen, out-of-date clothing, hoopskirts and corsets, yellowed towels with the Biltmore Hotel name, the shredded remains of a bankbook, a model of a racing barque with its sails and rigging at half mast. Here the faint scent of lavender and cedar lingered among the acrid dust of rat droppings and the sweet ammoniac odor of bats. His ear to a beam, Eichhorn could hear the tantalizing murmur of bat voices. This was their time of day. Without song or plumage they lacked the soft charm of feathered things. He could see in memory the bats swooping spasmodically over the barbed wire, and the prisoners, in those last starving days, weakly flinging stones at them in the hope of adding substance to their gruel.

Repelled when a bat detached itself from a rafter near the chimney shaft to hurl itself like a torn scrap of carbon paper into darker shadows, Eichhorn descended to the second floor. Here was another stairway, a smaller one than the one he had taken before. It went down into a kitchen that was redolent with dire smells. He remembered it well from the camps: excrement made sweeter still by the aroma of decomposition. His head reeled. He saw dead faces, nameless faces, then his mother staring back from haunted eyes, a band of reprieved prisoners playing *The Blue Danube,* and the dogs, those he had trained, standing stiffly beyond the wire, waiting for someone to run.

Both hands pressed hard against the stained enamel of the kitchen table, he tried to collect himself. He did not like this place at night. For the first time his resolve wavered, and he considered leaving. Should he go back up to the second floor, retrace his steps? No, he could not go back to that memory-laden labyrinth. The kitchen windows were barred with two-by-fours nailed across them. There were three doors in the kitchen in addition to the one leading to the backstairs. He hesitated, breathing through his mouth, his head lowered. His listened and heard nothing, and still the conviction deepened. He was not alone.

Tensed for confrontation, Eichhorn opened the first door. He cried out as an ironing board sprang at him from a cupboard. Still trembling, he tried the second door. It was nailed shut. The third led to the central hallway where he had begun his explorations. He could leave now, leave it for the boys in the lab to work out, or the bungling police,

121

or fate, or he could go to the end, to the narrow door that stood ajar, the one that led to the cellar. With the kerosene lamp held high he stood before the door and the newly scrawled legend, FATHER'S PLACE. The spray can of paint rolled on the floor at his feet. Eichhorn took a deep breath and slowly opened the door. He could see nothing. There was a putrid smell of decay. A battlefield smelled that way in summer. The camps in Poland had smelled that way in the end. As his eyes adjusted he became aware of roving shadows, and then something darker than the shadows, moving almost imperceptibly across the cellar floor, angling toward him. A heavy pulse beat in his ears like a clock, telling him the moments were passing. The darkness gave back two points of light, eyes with a cold malice he had seen before only in the SS corps that had patrolled the wire.

Another man might have retreated, slammed the door, but it was not Eichhorn's nature to retreat. There had been too much of that. He held the lantern steady in his left hand and curled the right more firmly around the ax handle. "You," he whispered in German, "come. We're still a family. Come, my babies." The ax was cocked back in his fist and the knotted muscles of his body were tense with expectation. His face was set, teeth bared, the tendons of his neck standing out like iron rods. He blew a long strident whistle, then paused. It would have brought them once, bounding with lolling tongues. "Come, my babies. It is only Eicchi. Come."

From below there was an ugly grating noise like the passage of two rough surfaces over each other. He saw again the glint of eyes, green and radiant as they reflected the lantern light, and in those blazing eyes he saw his doom.

122

These could not be the dogs he had raised on his own. He took a step down, feeling a blind fury rising within him, a fury of fear and disappointment. The ax was poised, yet to his horror, cutting through that fury, Eichhorn felt a kinship with the creatures waiting there, a bond of blood. He knew, and they knew.

A dark shape detached itself from the mass of shadows and moved steadily forward as though bidden. Slowly, even reluctantly, the form advanced to greet him. The lamplight flickered on something metallic. Then there came a headlong rush so that Eichhorn scarcely had time to interpose the ax, let alone wield it for a blow.

He felt blinding pain as though a giant fishhook had been thrust into his good leg, his arm, right through the heavy padding, drawing him down with an adamant and steady force into the loamy den. There was scarcely a struggle. Even if given the chance to use the ax, he might never have done so, and now the ax was rattling to the floor below. After it went the lantern, bursting into incandescence so that he seemed to see the devouring furnaces of Auschwitz. The world was ending in flames as he had always known it would. He meant to say, "It's not your fault," but the blood from the wound in his throat made bubbles in his mouth. Now there was a roaring and a flaming inside him, and everything was going black as though he had stared too long at the sun.

17

▼▼▼

After the angry congestion at the Village Hall, both Cathy and her father yearned for fresh air. A walk would help them wind down.

"But is it a good idea?" Cathy asked.

"It's a stupid idea, I suppose, but there is this," Jim said, hauling an old Mauser rifle out of its case. He had put on the heavy fisherman's sweater and a pair of high, laced hiking boots. The combination gave him a look of rustic authority.

"I hope we're taking the dogs," she said.

"Of course," Jim replied, putting bullets in the rifle, going against everything he had just said. "But leashes, mind. At least for the start."

It was immediately clear from Reveille's attentions that Taps was coming into heat. Still the bitch was having none of his adorations just yet, and with a growl she delivered a mock bite to his throat. There was probably not another unspayed female left in Sandy Cliffs, and not that many unaltered males to do anything about it. Jim smiled to himself; maybe that was what they meant by "a dog's life."

The two dogs seemed to sense that this was not a common walk and they lolled out their long pink tongues, sensing adventure. With their leashes attached their jaws quivered, ready to bark.

"Just slam the door, Cat. The catch is on."

The porch light made the hard white frost on the lawn glitter like diamonds. Such a coating took a clear footprint, and there were none ahead. By now the sickle moon was in the west, but the stars sparkled as they fled from one another with fearful speed.

Perhaps it was ill advised, but at the foot of the hill they let the dogs go free. Father and daughter watched them tear off, Jim saying, "Cry 'havoc,' and let slip the dogs of war."

"Shakespeare again," Cathy said. She'd been plowing through the Bard of Avon, more plays than Berkshire would have dared assign, and enjoying them.

Jim nodded. "If there's anything up ahead, we'll have ample warning from those two."

Taps led the way with an effortless yet oddly stiff-legged, wolfish gait that caused her to run almost sideways for a dozen steps or more.

"Do you really think there's some kind of weird superdog on the loose?" Cathy asked.

"Lord, I hope not," her father replied, for if there was he had come close to making a public pledge to track it down.

"Hey, what's that?" Cathy was pointing through the dark

125

grid of the last trees before the meadow opened wide. She answered her own question. "It's a fire!"

If anything had to burn, she hoped it was one of the new houses that recently had come to encroach upon the vanishing solitude of the Cooper beach. "We'd better call—" and just as she said it the alarm siren sounded in Port Monroe, routing out the volunteers.

Once out on the meadow road, they knew it had to be the old Van Rath farmhouse. The Sandy Cliffs Historical Society had hoped to restore it some day. A chorus of sirens that prickled the hair on the back of her neck told Cathy that the fire trucks were on the way.

"Not a chance of saving it," Jim said. "Too bad."

They watched from the meadow bridge. The windows were by now all aflame. The fire, spreading higher, seemed a violent pink in the night and cast down reflections of oily pinkness on the streams in the marshland. It was so still they could hear the pulsating roar. Saturated with salt from countless easterly storms, the roof bloomed incandescent, crumbled. Embers drifted over the neglected orchard and the ruined barn where the first black antic figures of the firemen danced against the glow.

"Did we ever take you over there, Cat?" She shook her head. "I went over a few times when I was a kid. They gave me fresh milk, right from the cow. I even rode their old plow horse. I hate to see the old place go." Even abandoned, the Van Rath farm had remained for Jim a signpost of the past and of what seemed to him a simpler, more bucolic, honest, and natural way of life. He remembered the black cows grazing in a green meadow. Now with a dull rumble the house sank in a red ruin. Sparks swirled upward, seeming to diminish the stars.

Slowly the flames fell back. Cathy and her father, the dogs at their feet, remained transfixed. The last farmhouse in Sandy Cliffs had vanished before their eyes.

As the fire began to gutter, the setting moon seemed to brighten, like the clipping of a finger nail imbedded in the solid sky.

"The moon, and then what?" Cathy said, breaking the spell.

"Stars."

"And then?"

"Nothing, I suppose. Infinity. Everlasting night."

"Makes me cold," she said.

Jim put his arm around her. "Let's head on back." Only madmen were said to linger in the moonlight.

As they started slowly back along the meadow road, Jim said, "I guess it's the fire . . . that place over there. I mean, I suddenly seem to need a confessor, Cat. I'm afraid that's you."

Sensing this was no light matter, Cathy paused. "You don't have to go into whatever it is, Dad, unless you want to."

But Jim was launched. "When you were a kid, I used to take on a few criminal cases. One of them was the Van Rath boy, just back from Vietnam. When he'd been over there he'd used a lot of flamethrowers. The evidence from the Army was that he torched a river community or two, houses, people, their boats. Without orders. Not long after he got back home, a boatyard in Port Monroe went up in flames. Lots of nice Chris Crafts and Hinkleys. The powers-that-be in the yachting fraternity weren't exactly delighted when I took the case and a lot less happy when I won it. To tell you the truth, I've kind of backed away from criminal cases ever since."

It had all seemed so clear-cut in law school: justice, pure and unquestioned, a fine distinction refined through the fires of legal controversy, but it never, in fact, seemed to work that way. The jury, in the end, sometimes chose the best liar or the most entertaining attorney.

"I don't get the connection, quite," Cathy admitted.

"The connection is that the defendant was guilty as hell, if a person who's insane is ever guilty under the law. He wasn't on the loose six weeks before another boatyard went up."

Cathy stopped walking for a moment. "And then his parents were found dead and he vanished," Cathy filled in, remembering spooky stories she'd heard over the years.

"I recall a little conversation with the mayor, not Kingston, the one before him. He said to me, 'You know, Jim, nobody's accusing you.' He meant that as reassurance, but of course I was accused. It isn't a very good idea to get on the bad side of the yacht club society in this county." All this Jim dropped quite casually, like a secret too old to keep.

"So that's why you were never offered a judgeship," Cathy said, more to herself than to Jim. "And I suppose that's why you keep telling me to be a judge."

"In part, yes, Cat." Jim sighed. "If you look at it as pure selfishness."

There didn't seem much more to say. Cathy took her father's arm. The night was cold, and she yearned for the warmth of home. "Come on, you dogs." The pair had never moved but gazed across the meadow to where the fire still flickered. Jim gave a sharp whistle, and suddenly they were all eager obedience.

"We'll have to keep Taps penned up for a while now," Cathy said. "Don't you think so, Dad?"

"Or every dog in the neighborhood will come baying at the door," Jim agreed.

On reflection, it might have been a mistake to take Taps along even now, and it occurred to her to ask, "Dad, you aren't treating Taps as bait or something, are you?" She felt a sudden lurch of fear in her stomach. Why hadn't she thought of this before?

Jim's reply was noncommittal. "The kennel's good and strong. We can go over the fence just to make sure."

Cathy slowly realized something irreversible had happened. They had left a double scent trail for over a mile, and she knew that a dog's sense of smell was beyond human appreciation. As long as a soaking rain did not intervene, a good tracking dog could follow a three-day-old trail unerringly, even if it was overlaid by the passage of hundreds of other creatures. Dogs could take these countless mingled odors and analyze and isolate one from all the rest. She and her father might just as well have stretched a red ribbon behind them. The thought was ominous, but it did not seem as dire as it should have. Omens are those messages from the future that are acknowledged only when the future slides into the past.

"Lord, where have all those stars come from?" Jim asked her. It was an absurd question; the same stars had been there for millions of years, but in the clear and icy darkness of that late autumn night it seemed as though new galaxies had blossomed in the sky.

"Maybe, Dad, we shouldn't feed the dogs as much as usual," she said. "Maybe they'd sleep less and keep better watch."

"Good thinking," Jim agreed. For once they seemed to understand each other.

18

▼▼▼

On December 18, Cathy woke with the knowledge that today they would be meeting Pat at the airport. She
conscientiously avoided exploring her feelings on that subject. Outside, the dogs were already barking. They were
always up early, and why not? After their breakfast they
went right back to sleep. Downstairs the old Chauncy
Jerome mantle clock made its brisk pronouncements:
Seven o'clock. Springs clicked and the little mallet tensed
itself for a future hour. Time to unbar the castle and let
down the drawbridge.

"Cat, what can I fix you for breakfast?" Jim was already
in the kitchen and a bit too cheerful, she felt.

"Nothing. I'll get it." That meant toast smeared with
margarine and a diet Coke.

"Cath, if I leave you to your own devices, you'll eat
enough junk to give a pig pimples. Let me fix you some
eggs."

130

"Cholesterol? Do you want to give me a heart attack?" To placate him she poured out a glass of orange juice, ostentatiously swallowed a vitamin pill. "Sorry," she said a moment later, "that didn't come out right." They had received the autopsy report on Joan: heart failure, death by natural causes, a conclusion nearly two weeks in coming.

Although Joan's body had been cremated at the hospital, something more had to be done. They had considered a memorial service at the local funeral parlor, but one visit had made up their minds. The place had been fitted out like a cheap cocktail lounge, with soft music wafting lugubriously from hidden speakers. "No, thanks," Cathy had spoken both their minds. They had attended a brief service at Brightsides, where a matron distracted Cathy by conscientiously plumping out her white nylon sleeves and an attendant kept coughing and sucking noisily on what she assumed were cough drops. She and her father had waited uneasily for the last strains of the organ so they could leave the horrible place and transport Joan's ashes to the rapidly expanding cemetery in Port Monroe. There Cathy found herself standing rigidly, imagining herself about to repose there in the ground forever, as her mother was about to do. She was beyond sorrow, was beginning to accept her mother's death; that is, it had begun to move from the present into the past, beyond denial.

"No more funerals for me, except my own, and maybe not that one," she told her father fiercely when it was all over. That had been a week ago, just after the Van Rath fire.

Before they drove to pick up Pat at the airport, Cathy went to the kennel, which was now divided into two separate runs with enclosed wooden structures built up against the house wall. Taps and Reveille faced her, their muzzles thrust against the stout wire mesh in jubilant anticipation of a walk, an event more treasured than food.

"Sorry, guys," she told the dogs. She had come with a hammer, a staple gun, and Jim's Mauser rifle, which frightened her, though she dared not tell him so. Great uncle somebody or other had brought it back from World War One. "Belleau Wood, June 1918" was cut into the wood of the gunstock. The bayonet, newly polished, was in place, and the gun loaded. With a great deal of uneasiness Cathy had learned how to load it, but she had not yet discharged a shot.

In the few minutes before they had to leave for Kennedy airport she went over the cyclone fence, old wire salvaged from her grandfather's tennis court but strong still, each separate link one sixteenth of an inch thick. Her father would undoubtedly have said something like, "They don't make wire like that anymore." She had to admit she had found no weak spots, but just to be sure she used the staple gun and hammer to secure the wire to the supporting posts, rather enjoying her skill at the task.

Taps and Reveille kept pace with her, rearing up now and then with their forelegs pressed against the mesh. There was a curious instant, during which they were still silent but about to protest their confinement, when Cathy became so acutely aware that they had the capability of being dangerous that the expectation of being bitten filtered through the intervening wire as though it were a sieve. She had to physically shake off the feeling, saying "Okay, you guys, settle down." In disappointment their heads arched back to howl as she hoisted the gun to her shoulder, grenadier style. Somehow it was easier to make a joke of it than accept what she really felt, that an eye was on the Cooper house, scrutinizing it.

Noticing that the little red flag was up, Cathy marched on to the mailbox: More catalogues, already announcing post-Christmas bargains. *Newsday* had finally picked up on the Van Rath fire with an eye-catching photograph of a human foot protruding, cracked, yet shiny as coal, from the rubble. The corpse had been identified only to the extent that it was not Jared Van Rath. With it had been found the bodies of two enormous dogs, also badly burned but evidently both female. Was this the end of the "Sandy Cliffs Horror?" speculated the article.

In with the rest of the mail, evidently broken open and resealed by the post office, was a small parcel addressed jointly to Cathy and her father. It came from Brightside and the handwriting was disturbingly familiar. She handed it to Jim and went on to transfer the dogs from the kennel to the house, confining Taps to the kitchen and giving Reveille the run of the place.

Apprehensively Jim tore open the package and, like so much excelsior, letters, smudged pastel sketches, poetry, poured out, the final siftings of Joan's room.

Old stuff. He scanned a poem dated June 1.

> From the dark Tower which is a ship's mast
> the stroke of one slips down through the night
> like the body of one drowned.
> On the blackboard the stroke of one inscribes its
>   scrawl.
> Glass-eyed houses dive into the night.
> Tails between their legs, the prowling dogs
> howl at the stroke of one as at a dead man.

133

The usual gloom. Jim might have set the rest aside had not the next item borne a date placing it after Thanksgiving, on the eve of Joan's death. This he read quickly, then a second time more slowly. When Cathy reappeared he handed it to her.

"Not now, Dad. We're late." She had given up on her mother's letters long ago.

"I think you should read it, Cat, while we drive."

At first Cathy focused only on the handwriting, more like printing, the straight, sturdy columns of *L*s and *T*s, the crosses often forgotten, then a snatch here and there. Matilda, a fellow patient, had stolen Joan's beloved copy of *Green Mansions,* devouring all but the binding. "I have wasted far too much time in this postgraduate university," Joan wrote. "That is how I have always deluded myself, but of course I know better. I know how the chronic patients pile up in the back wards, growing old where there is nothing but bare walls and the smell of bodies rotting. Here people become mushrooms and toadstools while I'm a walking percolator and exist in a state of perpetual anxiety. How many years ago was I painting along the banks of the Seine, little imagining I would be locked under custodial care with keepers and nurses? Too long. It is time to face reality. Last night was the first snow here and now it makes me yearn to be home for Christmas, home for good.

"Darlings, may I confess something? I feel somehow closer to you now on paper than I did before I left. Isn't that strange? I feel suddenly much better. I used to suspect there was no such thing as sanity for any of us. Now I realize as I sit by the window how mad I was. It is a quiet, gray day with just a trace of that snow on the ground. It would be nice to have a fire and some sherry. Such days always

134

make me think of Paris, the soft gray light, wisps of smoke from crooked chimneys. Escapist's thoughts, I agree. Oh put them behind me, Satan." Here Cathy sensed her mother was drifting back into poetry. "An end to delicacy, Angels rip through the air lassoing souls like cowboys. An end to fearfulness, hurricanes reward the brave with the sight of their quiet eye. An end to medication. I have hidden in the past too long. Yes, I do mean to come home for good. I really do mean for good. Sorry, I do mean to go on painting, trying to make the brush behave even if I am not that good at it. I no longer expect to change even one little corner of the world for the better. So you shall have to indulge my painting but, I promise, no more suicide attempts. Psychiatry is life without poetry, and I have been in it up to my ears. No more living in a dream world. It's reality for this kid. Septic tanks are seeping. Sewage is a-creeping. Jet fumes descending. Pollution never ending. Auto horns demanding. Freeways all expanding. Joan Cooper intends to learn to love it all.

"You can't imagine how brave I feel. There's a nurse, I don't know her grievance, but every single morning she confronts me with the same question. 'Tell me, Mrs. Cooper, are you winning or losing?' It used to make me cry, but now I just tell her, 'Winning, Mrs. Mendez. No question, I'm winning.' So, *mes chers,* write when you can. Life's an amazing thing, and I love to hear what you are doing about it. All love, Joan."

"Well, what do you make of that, Cat?" Jim said when she had refolded the letter.

"Mom, forgive me," Cathy replied. "I can't even cry." Did her mother's confidence spring from the safe presentiment of her imminent death? Or did she really mean it, about coming home and facing reality? Even if Joan believed it, could she possibly have coped with the demands of real life? Of course now the questions were sadly academic and yet somehow the letter had brought Cathy a measure of relief, as though she were being forgiven from beyond the grave.

They finally arrived at the airport and joined the endlessly circling traffic. Jets were streaming in and out steadily like wasps to a hive, leaving greasy smudges in the sky. By the time Jim had found a parking place and they entered the International Arrivals terminal, they were half an hour late for Pat's flight. Passengers flopped in molded plastic chairs, surrounded by the messy heaps of their carry-on luggage, awaiting the whims of higher gods. A stooped elderly man, gazing up at the television panel showing flights, soothed his frail wife. "They carry millions of people every day. It's safer than climbing out of the tub." "You know I can't get out of the tub," the woman replied with irritation.

The board indicated that Pat's flight was delayed. Jim couldn't get through the crowds at the information counter to ask, but rumors spread that the flight had been diverted to Boston. Then abruptly the enigmatic electronic pronouncement changed to "Arrived," and just as unexpectedly there was Pat, shoving a cart full of luggage through the customs gate.

Cathy recognized the striding walk first, then the high cheekbones, vaguely Slavic, with a peach-and-apple tint. Pat must have noticed them in the same instant. She waved, gazing over the crowd with sparkling if somewhat red-rimmed eyes.

"You guys look well," she called out in a husky voice.

"I should hope so, having you back again," Jim answered.

They stood a moment face to face. Cathy felt an odd, uncertain smile infuse her entire face. Then the three rocked together, a very fond embrace. Finally Pat pulled back, saying, "I'm surprised how much I missed you two. I really am."

"So," Jim said, gathering up her suitcases, "how was Milan?"

"Awful. Everyone was worrying about fallout, so there weren't any fresh vegetables, no salad, even though this time of year most of that stuff wouldn't even come from Europe. And then the pollution was so bad I began to lose my voice; between the smog and the rain and the fact that the *pensione* was freezing cold, it's a wonder I didn't get pneumonia. I missed two performances and of course didn't get paid for them. Between that and the tax cut the Italians took, I just about broke even."

"Otherwise, how did it go?" Jim asked as they waited at the traffic light to cross to the parking lot.

"Good reviews, I think. Singing in Italian is one thing; reading their newspapers is another." She laughed. "Good grief, it's cold here."

Jim was loading the suitcases into the trunk when Pat asked, "By the way, how's Joan? When is she coming home?" There was no immediate answer as Jim continued shifting her luggage around in the trunk. "Jim?"

"Joan's dead," he said, slamming down the trunk lid.

"What? How? Oh, Jim, I would have come back," Pat protested.

"It was right after you got to Italy," Cathy interrupted. "Dad and I talked it over, and we knew you were doing something important."

"There wasn't anything you could have done, Pat," Jim said.

"But Joan's been gone nearly three weeks and I didn't even know," Pat lamented. She took a deep, tremulous breath and began to sob.

"Come on, Cat, let's get this jet-lagged lady home," Jim said, opening the car door. "Give her some Kleenex." He wanted to get the drive and the explanation of how Joan had died over with quickly, but it had begun to rain, a cold steely rain that splintered on the windshield. With visibility impaired, expressway signs loomed out of the darkness with their terse commands: No Stopping, Construction Ahead, Squeeze Left. The traffic began to slow, became stop-and-go.

Pat was still crying, though more quietly. With her laryngitis, the long flight, and now tears, her eyes were as red as her nose, and all her dignity had been abdicated. "Listen, you two, you don't need me cluttering up the place just now," Pat said. "If I were . . ."

"We do," they both insisted, cutting her off.

"Now, listen. You guys ought to clear out. Go to the Bahamas, St. Thomas, something entirely different," Pat persisted.

"I wish we could," Jim agreed.

"All three of us," Cathy added diplomatically.

"But the truth is, we've got a mess in Sandy Cliffs," Jim explained. "As a village official, I can't duck it just now."

The stream of cars finally began to move at a normal speed. An overturned tractor-trailer proved the cause of the delay. A dog had somehow strayed onto the road, and in applying its brakes the truck had overturned. The dog had vanished entirely except for one paw that protruded from beneath the wreck, as firmly pinned as the Wicked Witch of the West beneath Dorothy's house and as dead as the array of marbled beef carcasses that had cascaded from the tractor-trailer to glisten in the headlights.

Cathy briefly brought the new arrival up to date, concluding, "So there you have it, *The Sandy Cliffs Horror* in living color.

"And I thought Europe had problems," Pat replied, her emotions now under control.

"Most people think the fire at Van Rath's finished whatever it was," Cathy added, "but I'm still going around with that gun."

"Come on," Pat protested. "Jim, she's got to be kidding. Cathy's carrying a gun?"

"Not kidding at all," he said. "It's still news." He turned on the radio, which announced with urgency that there were only six more shopping days until Christmas. Then came a long-range forecast of unseasonably warm weather followed by a cold front and the possibility of a white Christmas. "Wish it would snow," he said, realizing that a good snow cover might help resolve the still unanswered questions in Sandy Cliffs.

From the radio came the results of a laboratory study indicating that an increased population density made for aggressive behavior and cannibalism among rats. Finally, after the announcement of a nursing home fire in Newark that had taken untold lives, there was an update on the Van Rath fire. The human remains had been positively identified as those of a Paul Eichhorn, a former employee of the U.S. Army and once associated with the Nazi SS. Had he survived, the announcer speculated, he might have faced extradition as a war criminal. A congressman had asked for an investigation. A second, as yet unidentified corpse had been found.

"Nice little Sandy Cliffs," Pat said. "I always thought it was so peaceful, coming out here from the city."

Following the news came a broadcast of Christmas carols, and as the three drove to the waiting house they were silent, lulled by all the talk of wise men, guiding stars, and love.

19

▾ ▾ ▾

A day of brief Indian summer followed the rain. It flushed the last few sailboats out onto the bay, summoned tennis players and a handful of golfers at the Sandy Cliffs Club. The last of these lingered as long as the light allowed, though by four-thirty the clubhouse windows glowed brighter than the sky, inviting them back from hard play to the weary laughter of the bar and lounge. For those with children, the annual visitation of Santa Claus would take place in the main dining room.

A vivid sunset reflected on the bay. Along the blazing ridge of the seventeenth hole a golf cart moved, laborious as a white beetle. The air, with its dash of winter spice, was enough to make an old man feel young, and Frederick Bennett, Sr., whose face still slumped off center like a weary balloon from the effects of a near-fatal stroke, could fill his lungs with adolescent reassurance and feel fleetingly more hale than the fragile absurdity of his parts.

His companion and regular opponent was Frederick, Jr. Fred and Freddie, two generations of Harvard men, both sporting heavy crimson sweaters emblazoned with a modest *H*. Here the resemblance ceased. Freddie was considerably taller than his father, a long, ungainly strider, pink and unblemished as a gigantic kewpie doll when he stood under the clubhouse shower, an indulgence that just now had great appeal.

The sun lay on the horizon pierced by its own crimson spears, bleeding from every artery, and Freddie would happily have aborted the game for that hot shower, followed by the solace of a very dry Gibson and the innocent delights of the children's Christmas party.

The only regret of his bachelorhood was having no children of his own, and were it not a village tradition for the mayor to play Santa Claus, Freddie would have volunteered for the job.

"Why don't we head on in, Pop?" he suggested.

"Without a winner?" replied the old man suspiciously.

"Happy to concede," Freddie offered, but his father believed in finishing what he had begun, particularly when that involved winning, and it was not too dark for Freddie to notice the older man teeing up his ball on the fairway.

As his own game improved and his father's declined from what had been a commendable eight handicap, a silent conspiracy had grown between them. The old man must go on winning, for to do so was to repudiate his mortality. If this altered the objective of the play, it did call for increasing ingenuity on Freddie's part and gave support to his cheerful conclusion that the world was a fraud and mankind a species to be manipulated.

"Good show, Pop," Freddie observed as his father sent

the ball top-spinning a hundred yards down the course and into the rough. His own ball already lay on the green, and he would have an amusing time piling up the putts. Otherwise, he would hear complaints all evening about the liabilities of getting old. So they motored on, quite unconscious that their scent had been trapped, analyzed, and was now being followed with the clarity of a searchlight, or that their pursuer was narrowing the gap with long undulant strides. Against the sky, drained finally of its fire to become a suboceanic green, the golf cart moved painfully toward the seventeenth green.

Two more bounding shots brought the senior Bennett to the edge of the green. "Perhaps we should skip the eighteenth," Freddie suggested hopefully.

"Nonsense." His father ended the discussion as usual.

Freddie had just brought the golf cart to a halt when he heard a rustle of rapid motion and saw something approaching. In and out of the shadows, its coat glistened briefly like wet leather as it came on with relentless speed. Freddie had only time enough to say, "Dad, let's get this thing going," when his trouser leg was shorn away at the knee and he felt the welling up of hot blood along his calf. His father had begun shouting incoherently and waving a mashie niblick. Both men clung to the cart, which scuttled onto the green itself.

"Faster, for God's sake!" the older man urged, the club raised ax fashion in both hands above his reverted head.

Then the cart swerved, pitching into the inky pool of a sand trap. Freddie sprawled onto the edge of the green, not six feet from where his ball lay, an easy putt from the hole. He had the bewildered thought, "How can I miss and make it look good?" before remembering that the game was

143

over. Something he had not really seen was trying to kill him. Without a thought for the chairman of the board, he made a blinding, pain-ridden scramble to escape.

Fred Bennett, Sr., had stayed with the cart. Now he found himself down on all fours, sand in his mouth. As he tried to rise, something bowled him over, seemed to sink great barbs into his thigh. Still he crawled through yielding sand to the trap's lip, flung one hand over onto the cut grass, then the other, gained the rim, poised there for an instant, and after a heartbeat of time released a terrible howl of fear, agony, and disbelief before being drawn inexorably down into the black sandy crater.

Meanwhile, summoning all his strength, Freddie ran toward the glitter of the clubhouse. He dragged one leg clumsily, using both hands to help it work. His lungs ached. Glancing over his shoulder, he stumbled, knocking so hard against a beech tree that he pirouetted around, fell to his knees, then limped on again under a sky that had yielded up its gold and green to brown wisps of city poison.

With his objective but a short sprint away, Freddie fell again, laboriously as a circus elephant settling its haunches, just as a projectile overtook him and he was down with his face in the leaves. He felt no additional pain, only an intense surprise and a violent jolting back and forth as though his nemesis meant to shake the stuffing out of him. He lay there, head cradled in his arms, waiting for another attack. His legs felt warm and sticky from the bleeding. In the gathering dusk the blood seeped out, oily and black.

When no assault came, Freddie rose painfully, limping toward the club. He was near enough to see the Christmas tree lights through the window and hear the laughter of children, near enough to shout, "Someone help me!" for he knew without looking back that he was being overtaken again. "Oh, God! Help me!" but there was no one to help as the terrible jaws found his throat. He, Freddie Bennett, graduate of Harvard Business School, major in the field artillery reserve, junior partner at Bennett, Bradshaw, and Hinman, was being ravaged like a rag doll.

In the clubhouse a score of golfers occupied the lounge bar with its eastern exposure. The windows fronting on the eighteenth green had gone black. They were swapping weekend gossip. One pair played backgammon, double six. Exclamations came from the dining room next door where children, crowded around the Christmas tree, were being given small gifts by a plump Santa, with promises of more lavish ones when the big day arrived.

Then the outer door burst open and Freddie Bennett stood in the frame. Mayor Kingston would later relate that it was the worst thing he had ever seen.

Freddie dragged himself into the center of the lounge. He was safe now, among friends. He must warn them. His tongue pressed through steel-gray lips. "Aaah," he muttered, "Aaah," staring about with wild blue eyes.

"My God, who is it?" someone exclaimed.

Legs dragging like sandbags, Freddie propelled himself across the room, heading toward the dining room. He had already gained the doorway before Mayor Kingston shouted, "Not in there! Not with the kids!" but it was the kids Freddie meant to warn. He tried to speak, but the wound made thick bubbles in his mouth. His tongue protruded, vibrant, followed by a flush of blood. His knees gave way and he fell, hands fluttering with a life of their own as he lay there.

"Get the kids out of here!" the mayor directed, a pillow

he did not require sliding from beneath his red jacket. Some of the smaller children were screaming; others looked back and forth with disturbed, hopeful smiles. What was Santa up to? What sort of Christmas prank was this? "For God's sake, will somebody call an ambulance? Freddie, just hang on. We're getting a doctor." For some reason Harry Kingston had it in his stubborn head that you could talk a man back to life.

"He's gone," the bartender said, standing up. He wiped his hands on his white jacket, leaving red smears. "Can you believe all that blood from just one body?"

They stood there, children, Santa Claus, and all, fascinated, horrified. Santa tore off his beard to the further consternation of his bewildered audience and shouted, "Don't panic!" in a falsetto voice. He upset a highball glass, which broke, tinkling, on the polished slate floor. "And somebody lock that door." He then misdialed the police station, hung up on his startled wife, dialed again.

Not until Chief Mahoney stood in the club's parking lot with the force's one riot gun did anybody start for home. There was no speculation upon the whereabouts of the senior Bennett until much later, when his wife telephoned the club. Even then, he was not found until the following morning, and then purely by accident, so thoroughly had he become one with the sand.

20

▼▼▼

Sandy Cliffs, despite publicity that rivaled Iraq's new concussion bomb exploded over Iran, girded for a white Christmas. The last commuter train was safely berthed in Port Monroe. No snow had yet fallen, but a sky of cast iron and a cold wind from the east breathed a warning from winter that promised to confirm the forecast.

Inside the Cooper home, perhaps as a counterweight to all that had gone on, the holiday was being overstressed—holly and strands of balsam draped around the chandelier in the hall, spilling red and green from the mantle below the portrait of Judge Cooper, who glared down with perpetual disapproval, red and green for Cathy, Jim, and Pat, and for Bruce, who was expected to share part of the evening with them.

To Cathy the old house had never looked so festive. The mincemeat pies were made, the gifts wrapped. The tree lights worked on the first try. Despite the trace of haunted pallor that she saw in mirrors, she felt in herself a new repose. Her heart was still distracted, but her nerves were finally at peace. As long as the tree glowed in the hall, she felt a link with holidays past and a sense of anniversary she experienced at no other time. Something lost had been returned to the house, and there was a sense of life as fleeting and warm as laughter. As long as the tree stood, life would be protected, even in the dark of the year. Other forces seemed to enter the house with the tinsel and the glow; they were good and loving, guardian angels.

Bruce arrived in late afternoon. He was in high spirits, having just been presented with the club trophy for winning the autumn Frostbite sailing series. He placed the small silver bowl on the mantle, saying, "One of these days we'll win it together."

"I'm for that," Cathy agreed. Under the mistletoe they exchanged a kiss.

Then Jim appeared from outside with firewood. "Is that a gun I noticed in your car?" he asked Bruce.

"Just a twenty-two, sir," Bruce admitted.

"I'd keep it out of sight if I were you. The police have orders to confiscate toys like that. What do you plan on shooting with it, anyway?"

"I'm a pretty good shot, actually," Bruce said defensively.

"A gun like that's only good for tin cans," Jim told him.

Since the deaths on the golf course, hysteria in the village had reached a fever pitch. The second charred body in the farmhouse cellar had been positively identified as that of Jared Van Rath; his death was attributed to unknown causes sometime prior to the fire. With the inability of the local police force to cope with such events, the county had stepped in with various experts and additional men. Their first act had been to place a twenty-four-hour guard on the seventeenth hole, both to deter curiosity-seekers and in the hope that the perpetrator would return to the scene of the crime.

At a meeting earlier that day, Mayor Kingston had told Jim, "This business is more than I bargained for." Defeat was written in every crease in his clothing, in the limp hang of his jacket, the necktie knotted off center. Jim was alarmed at the sight of him.

"Harry," he said, "are you feeling okay?"

Kingston looked up and smiled, though a faint look of bewilderment stayed in his eyes.

"Mildred's trying to get us on a flight to Palm Beach," Kingston admitted. "It's a cowardly thing to do, but, Jim, I just may."

"I don't blame you," Jim said. "I may just hitch a ride." He did not intend to go that far, but for the sake of peace and quiet on Christmas Eve he had surreptitiously pulled out the master telephone jack in the basement.

While Taps had been allowed the run of the kitchen, where the air was redolent with the smells of sugar, butter, and flour baking together, Reveille had been relegated to the kennel. His doleful barks could be heard inside the house. "Poor old Rev," Cathy said and grabbed a sweater and two dog biscuits. The shepherd's face glowed satanic in the beam of her flashlight as she pressed a biscuit through the wire.

She heard a singing sound. A high wind was building. A dull yellow light brooded over the trees where the sky seemed to be descending. It was then that the first flakes fell. Cathy caught one on her tongue. It burned. The first

149

real snow of the year. This seemed to link all the times in her life. Now it was really Christmas.

"Cath? Hey, Cath, what are you doing out here?" It was Bruce.

"It's beginning to snow," she replied, as though no further explanation was necessary.

Even now the blizzard was moving majestically over Pennsylvania. It had begun slowing traffic on the Jersey Turnpike, yellowing barge lights on Chesapeake Bay, blowing inexorably over the Hudson and the East Rivers, shrouding the skyscrapers of Manhattan, and grounding planes at airports from Washington to Boston.

"I love it," Cathy exclaimed.

"And I love you," Bruce told her.

"I'm glad," she said, beaming at Bruce through the flakes. "You know, when it snows, it seems as if anything can happen so long as it snows hard enough. I mean nice things . . . and still, I have the weirdest feeling. Just look at Rev." The dog stood at the wire, staring intently into the screen of falling snow.

"Of being watched?" Bruce asked.

"Something like that," she agreed, taking his hand.

"Let's go inside," Bruce said, for it was the same eerie feeling that had sent him looking for Cathy in the first place.

21

▼▼▼

On the hearth the fire rose high. Hot buttered rum simmered before the blaze. With Bruce at the piano they ran through the usual carols. During the lulls Cathy heard now and then the forlorn barking of her dog.

Finally she told her father, "It's so cold, I think I'll take Rev a couple of blankets."

"Don't be silly. He's tough as an old boot," Jim replied.

They were well into the tongue-testing *Twelve Days* when Cathy quietly broke away. At the front door she paused, considered the rifle that stood there. No, it was only twenty quick steps to the kennel gate, and there she would be safe inside the wire with her old friend.

The kennel house with its swing door was really well insulated; it wasn't the cold that bothered Cathy but what she had to admit privately was the corny notion that on the first Christmas all the animals had been allowed into the manger. Rev heard her coming and stood with his forepaws

151

high on the fence wire. Between them the snow fell steadily, straight down in a great silence interrupted only by the foghorn sending forth its lonely warning on the Sound.

It was clear that ten days confinement in the kennel had not diminished Reveille's spirits. He greeted Cathy with wild delight, each joyous bark producing a puff of frosty breath. Paws on her shoulders, he thrust a moist muzzle into her face. His hot breath warmed her cheeks as his weight forced her a step backwards.

"Rev," she asked, "is that blood?" The left side of his lip was torn. Then she noticed that the wire mesh had been loosened from its anchoring frame. "Trying to break out, are you? That's not nice, and me bringing you these quality blankets. You just don't understand why you're locked up. We can't have you and Taps having puppies. Not right now. Maybe later." Like her mother, Cathy always talked to animals as though they had complete comprehension. Wasn't there some old folktale about animals having the gift of speech at Christmas? She liked to think so.

Reveille showed no such sudden talent, nor did he look interested in the blankets. He had returned to the wire with fixed attention, his ruff bristling. Something must be near, but Cathy heard not a sound besides the foghorn and the sibilant hiss of the falling snow. Yet as before there was a nebulous sense of intrusion. Cathy found herself casting about for a weapon. She cursed herself for not bringing the rifle, but a pitchfork leaned up against the shed. Feeling foolish, she took hold of it while telling herself, "What's the use in this, now the ground's frozen?"

Then Reveille began to growl, a deep, savage subterranean sound she had never heard before. With the dog's

152

sharp black muzzle as a compass, Cathy stared into the whirling white, saw a shadowy, formless thing beyond the range of identification, perceived dark motion, lost it in a blur of flakes, saw it again. Its whole body bore an affinity to shadow: The dark statue of a dog standing as a horse must stand that poses for heroic sculpture, implying not only weight and speed but a terrible determination to hunt and slay.

As Cathy watched, it moved forward, head down, imperceptibly at first, as flames breathe through dry leaves or a stone settles through clear water. Then it came faster, unswerving, silent as a ballet dancer, straight toward the kennel. Fifty yards now . . . Cathy thanked God for the fence, then remembered it had been loosened from its frame. She felt a dreamlike sense of unreality as her hands tightened on the pitchfork. "Hurry!" She had to instruct her hands, arms, legs what to do, had to fight that dispersion of consciousness that seemed as dangerous as the creature that hurled itself upon the wire without a sound. Even in her deadly peril, she registered what a splendid, terrible creature it was: Not as big as she might have dreamed it in nightmares but bigger than any dog she had ever seen. She could recognize the wolfhound and the Great Dane, and something more. At least three feet at the shoulder, big boned, heavy as a man and dark as gun metal.

The intruder and Reveille met at the wire. The former, programmed to kill, bored in silently, while Reveille screamed back through white teeth.

Cathy stood a moment, helpless witness to the frenzied scrabble of the two animals, holding back the scream that was rising in her. Then she remembered the pitchfork and thrust it toward the attacker, only to have it torn away by the lashing back and forth of the fence. She retrieved it in time to see the fence disintegrating amid the struggle, heard wood splintering.

All Cathy's vigor seemed to be streaming out in terror through the soles of her feet. With what seemed her last strength she dove for the swinging door into the shed, had a fleeting vision of both dogs inside the wire, locked in struggle.

Cathy told herself she was safe; there was nothing supernatural out there. The shed was stout. Her back braced against the far wall, she held the swing door with her feet. In a moment there was a sudden scrabbling at the door. She stiffened herself against the pressure, which relented in another flurry of combat outside, then silence.

Had they run off to fight elsewhere? It seemed to be over. Still fear spread through her body like brandy, numbing the nerve endings, infusing the muscles. It was as though the animal part below conscious control was taking over her body. "It's a bad dream," she told herself. "It has to be." Her mind withdrew into a trancelike state akin to sleep.

Cathy waited, counting the moans of the foghorn, thinking they seemed to come so quickly, wondering why she had not been missed. Of course the piano was at the far end of the house, and Pat had promised to sing some of the arias she had performed in Italy, and if Cathy had come to one conclusion about opera, it was that of volume. Still they must come soon—and, God knows, could be caught in the open. She had an intense feeling that something was waiting just beyond the door. "Dad?" she said. "Bruce? I'm in here!" This proved a signal for an assault on the shed door, which leapt and chattered in its frame. Without

154

a growl or bark the pounding came again so quickly that it seemed to Cathy impossible that only one creature was involved.

"I'm ready for you," Cathy told it. "Come on, damn you." The pitchfork was a claw that she held poised in the narrow passage, waiting, waiting as the heavy points began to droop until without warning the attack came again. Abruptly the shaft of the weapon was seized by a mouth full of fangs. Cathy tried to stab forward, then pull back. She felt the hot slick tongue on the back of her hand, the teeth sharp as polished nails grazed her wrist. Then the handle of the pitchfork jarred against her cheek, sent her sprawling into brief oblivion. She came to in painful confusion, aware of the hurt first and then the peril.

In the darkness Cathy groped for the pitchfork. Nothing. She was left with only bare hands. It seemed the sentence of doom had been pronounced and only the final execution remained. "This is it," she told herself. "This is it."

Then she heard a sound like thick sticks being broken, one after another, and she realized it was Bruce's little pump action .22. "Cath! Cathy! Where are you?" Bruce called out.

Cathy was not about to emerge from the shed, and Bruce had to overcome a pair of battering feet to open the door. "Cathy, Cathy, are you okay?" Her arms felt as though they had been yanked from their sockets and she had a bruise and swelling on her cheek—no serious injuries, but she was hysterical and crying as Bruce led her out. Jim and Bruce supported her to the front door, Bruce trying to calm her down with the palm of his hand stroking her head, as he would a dog.

"Jim, you should have let me have that," Pat said, nodding toward the Mauser, which he placed against the wall by the door. "I'd have nailed him." As a child she had gone coyote hunting with her father, delighting him with her unerring aim. She had hated the pointless slaughter more with every hunt, but it had seemed one way to win his approval, and that she had wanted desperately.

In the living room they were full of questions. "Mom was right," Cathy kept saying. "Mom was right." Still they asked her questions, even when she told them in her loudest voice to leave her alone. Finally nothing remained but to scream. She did not stop until she felt Bruce's hand clapped over her mouth. She bit down and he pulled away with a shout of pain and outrage, then shoved her down on the couch and pulled a lap robe over her.

Cathy, with little fight left in her, began to sob, knowing her beloved Reveille was dead somewhere and that the world was full of menace. Her mother had been right all along. Change was what killed; progress was only a degrading slide to something worse. With her eyes fast shut she willed the years away until her mother read again from *Llewelyn's Hound*. Even as she seemed to hear the words as from a dusty record under a needle, the poem soured, mocked her.

> But when he gained his castle door,
> aghast the chieftain stood;
> the hound all o'er was smeared with gore,
> his lips, his fangs, ran red.

The poem had made her cry at the time, that a faithful companion could be so ill-used. Now the words seemed a fearful prophecy. Slowly Cathy pulled the lap robe up over her head.

156

Pat sat down quietly beside Cathy. "Want to talk?" she asked. "Let me look at your arm." Cathy thrust out her scratched arm. "Skin's not broken, nothing to worry about," Pat said, but she wiped the mark with peroxide all the same. Still not a word from Cathy. "I was attacked once," Pat went on. "No, not by a dog. It was a person, someone for whom I'd have done anything. It was very horrible. I never really spoke to him again, and yet I still owe him something. He'd gotten me started with singing. I probably wouldn't be here now if he hadn't done something stupid that I expect he's regretted ever since. Funny, how life works out. . . ." Pat's voice trailed off. It was as though she had spoken more to herself than to the girl on the couch. Presently Pat stood up. "Well, listen to me, sounding like Miss True Confessions. Look, Cath, I'm going to see if things are burning up in the kitchen. Give a shout if you need anything. Your father and Bruce are outside . . . yes, they have both the guns. And, Cathy, you'll be fine. You're like me, a whole lot tougher than you think."

Cathy had heard all of Pat's words but made no reply. Presently, to drown her own thoughts, she turned on the stereo, thinking, "I suppose those two retards think they're being macho, looking for that thing."

Cathy was correct to the extent that Jim and Bruce were outside with flashlights and guns, but their search was over. They had found what they sought.

While Bruce had followed the tracks that led away into the woods, Jim had whistled for Reveille. Finally the moving beam of his flashlight had picked up something piled into the shadow of the woodpile. Already snow covered, the outline was clear enough.

"Ah, Rev," he called, and as he knelt down beside the

stacked wood, the last doubt was snuffed out. Reveille lay beside the logs as though he had been flung down out of the sky. His tongue lolled out, dry as a pink flannel rag.

Jim took hold of his old friend's head. "Rev?" There was no response, and from the loose motion of the neck Jim knew there never would be. A one-hundred-and-twenty-pound shepherd, not all that much past his prime, broken like a cheap toy.

It was not in the nature of an ordinary dog to do that sort of thing, Jim knew. Dogfights were for dominance and nothing more, and Reveille had clearly surrendered, exposing his throat and belly to his conqueror. That was where it should have ended, but here were gashes in the thick fur of Reveille's throat just behind the ears, as close to cold-blooded murder as a dogfight could be.

"My fault, boy," Jim told him. He had lured the damned creature here, sure as fate. He wondered if he had done it deliberately, thinking he could solve the problem, play God. And Cathy. He gave a shiver of fear, thinking it could have been her body flung down in the snow. Still he had lost Rev. That was the thing about dogs; they never did complain, never lamented their bad luck. The injustice of it was so complete, so one-sided, that in the privacy of the backyard Jim broke down and cried as he had not done since childhood, a hemorrhage of tears, for his dog, Joan, himself, the disastrous Midas touch that seemed to doom everything he tried to set right.

"Sir, I'm awfully sorry." He felt Bruce's hand on his shoulder and pulled himself together, even though he was too late to hide his weakness. "Don't mind me, sir. Tears are a good thing now and then."

But Jim was immediately all business. "Find anything?

And Bruce, please stop calling me 'sir.' It makes me feel ancient."

"Okay, sir. I'm afraid I lost the trail after a few yards, and not a trace of blood. I thought I was a better shot than that."

There seemed nothing more to do there. Jim found a tarpaulin in the garage and put it over Rev's body; then they went inside where Pat met them in the hall, a finger to her lips.

"How's she doing?" Jim whispered.

"Needs bucking up," Pat told them. "Let's see what Bruce can do."

"Oh, boy," he said. "I'm not really good at that sort of thing," but he went without hesitation and sat down beside the couch where Cathy lay. There was a painful silence during which he waited for her to break the ice, but when no response was forthcoming he finally said, "Is there someone under that blanket?"

"No. Go away."

Bruce wanted to say the right words of comfort but sensed that if he tried, he would say the wrong things and make matters worse. "Cathy, you know how sorry I am."

"Don't be sorry," from the blanket. "You're so awful when you're sorry."

Reaching over to turn down the stereo, Bruce asked her, "What are you doing under there?"

"Having a ball, can't you see that?" Cathy reached out an arm, turning the volume up even louder. "I know Rev's dead, you don't have to tell me. And that other thing?"

"Wish I knew," Bruce said, feeling suddenly terribly tired. He reached out and touched her hand. A strange sound, half laughter, half astonishment, as if surprised she

159

was really there, came from his lips. He pressed her hand and she covered his fingers with her own.

"Cathy, no matter what, being depressed on Christmas Eve is a punishable crime. Even first offenders are prosecuted. So smile? Just a little smile?" He pulled back the edge of the lap robe.

"Do you mind!" she said, pulling it back over her head.

"Aren't you suffocating under there? Come on, a teeny weeny little smile, and I'll let up on you.

"If you don't come out, I'll start tickling," he threatened.

"Oh, no you don't!" Cathy exclaimed as she emerged from the blanket. "I wish I could stay mad at you," she said, and a giggle forced itself to the surface.

"Seriously, how are you doing?" Bruce asked, and Cathy, just as serious, replied evenly, "I wish I knew."

"Don't be sad about Rev. You're lucky to be alive. That was one hell of a close call. Things could be worse."

"They could be a lot better." As Bruce put his arms around her he felt the convulsive movements of her body as she sobbed without making a sound. Presently the crying stopped. Cathy was like her father when it came to public emotion. "There," she said, "that's enough of that." She groped for a Kleenex in her pocket and produced a fair imitation of a foghorn.

"I think someone ought to call the cops," Bruce said, and Cathy agreed, but when Bruce made the attempt the phone was dead. Ten minutes after Jim's chagrined confession that he had unplugged the jack, three police cars slewed down the driveway. Following Jim's explanation, the cars took off for the beach road. Jim watched the fading taillights and wondered how, with the snow intensifying, they would ever find anything, let alone make it back up the hill.

"You know something funny?" Cathy said a few moments later. "The police came and went, and Taps didn't bark once."

They searched the house, but Taps had vanished. "I know I locked the kitchen door," Jim said, and whistled again for the dog. A second examination of the kitchen revealed the door to the old-fashioned milk closet ajar. A relic of the days of milkmen and their deliveries, the door led to a similar one outside. "She must have been frantic to get out to squeeze through such a small opening," Jim said. "What we need now is for someone to say it's all going to go away."

"All right, that's me," Pat volunteered, "because if all of you don't pitch in, this will be a Christmas Eve without a feast."

They all did try, but the festive mood was in shreds. Bruce remembered the hot buttered rum steaming beside the fire, and it seemed the stuff of holiday ambiance or, more truthfully, anesthesia. He handed Jim a mug of the dark brown brew of cider and rum.

"Why, thank you," Jim said absently. "This could be just what I need." He drank down one deliberate swallow after another, without feeling the scalding fluid pass his lips. Slowly in his mind a strengthening image began to form. The hunter's revenge? Not at all, but that of more hot buttered rum and a bowl of steaming, creamy clam chowder that Pat had just placed on the table.

Cathy shook her head at Pat's offer of chowder. Her stomach was still too fluttery for her to be hungry. She went to the front door and through the open crack whistled through the falling snow for Taps. Nothing. She leaned her forehead on the cold unyielding wood until Bruce came, gave a few strident whistles of his own, and then closed the

161

door hard until it latched. He led Cathy back to the dining room.

Presently Pat brought in the main course, saying, "It's supposed to be Szechuan, moo shu pork, actually. Not your standard Christmas dinner."

"This stir-fried stuff is outstanding," Bruce said. Both he and Pat were trying very hard.

Sensing this, Cathy began to rally. "You'll have to show me how you make this, Pat," she said after her first swallow. She was glad of Pat's choice of food; Chinese food was always so soothing.

"Under the circumstances, I hate to admit it but I'm starving," Pat said.

"If you'll cook like this, I wish you'd let me invite you out more often," Jim said, warmed by the rum. "In fact, I wish you'd stay for good."

The pie was also of Pat's making. It received praises all round the table, but she herself said the crust was not quite crispy enough, and Jim heard her with a smile in his mind if not on his lips.

He was about to propose a toast when the phone rang. "One more of Job's messengers," he said, but he jumped to catch it before anyone else moved. In the dark corner under the front stairs he bent and said hello. The others listened. "Is that you, Harry? . . . I thought you'd be in Palm Beach by now. Flights canceled? I see . . ." and then he was nodding silently, coming back with, "That's fine news. You say they have the body? . . . They don't? Now be honest, Harry. There are plenty of others to tell me lies. . . . Well, I hope you're right. We could do with a bit more proof . . . I know, I know. Merry Christmas to you, too, Harry."

He put down the phone, not quite sure if this was a new day or the shambles of yesterday. Returning to the table, from which came a babble of questions, Jim explained, "That was the mayor. He's heard from the police. They trailed the thing to East Creek, caught it in a crossfire. Only problem is, the tide took the body out to sea. Well, I guess it's over." He added uncertainly, "let's hope." He glanced over at Cathy and if eyes could make conversation they would have said, "but with Cooper luck, it'll turn out they shot Taps by mistake."

Bruce poured out hot buttered rum all around, warning Cathy, "This'll get to you quicker than you think."

Presently, as the house cooled, they moved back to the warmth of the fireplace. Peering out the window, Cathy said wistfully, "It looks like the start of another ice age." The storm let fall its infinite hissing flakes. By morning they would be buried, the deep freeze, no more worries. "Are you going to be able to get your car out, Bruce?" she asked; the snow was already drifting.

"No problem. I can always walk home if I have to," he said.

There seemed to Cathy something completely positive about the fireplace, deep, shadowy, and dark, seared by flames of long ago, so many warm memories, such a promise of warmth to come. For some time the group sat silent, gazing into the dazzle of firelight, enjoying the blues and greens from the driftwood. Jim squeezed Cathy's hand, fragile, thin-fingered, the incredible living flesh of a spirit existing outside himself, filled with hopes and fears and confusion, another vulnerable world he could never entirely enter. With this awareness came a wave of tenderness that he could never put into words, but that would lend support to the conviction that, if need be, the parent will die for the sake of the child.

"Now what's that noise?" Pat asked.

"The wind," Jim told her.

"And now. Is that the wind?"

"Just a branch on the shutters. Don't worry," Jim insisted. Cocooned in the warmth of family and fire, it seemed too unfair for an intrusion now, and yet finally he did get up and approached the front door. "All right," he asked, "who's there? Who wants to come in?" This was responded to by a heavy scraping noise, nothing more. Jim braced himself, his rifle at the ready while Bruce pulled open the heavy Dutch door. There behind the storm glass stood Taps.

22

▼▼▼

They toasted each other in the rosy glow of the firelight. Jim felt sleepy yet omnipotent, like a troll in a dream, capable of enormous strides and wall-shattering blows. With flamboyant grace, he stirred the embers.

"Don't get plastered," Pat whispered. "You'll spoil things."

What was there left to spoil, he wondered but replied, "Fear not, just enough to relax." Outside, fat flakes continued to fall. Sandy Cliffs was settling down into safe, banked drifts. When morning came children would go bursting out with their bright new sleds to climb the polar hills, hurtling down all day long until it was dinnertime again. So Jim imagined it.

There was no place in Jim's bright nostalgia for the dark storm outside or the wind-lashed tide that continued to ebb from East Creek. Flakes like feathers dissolved in the dark, murmuring current, which dimpled into fading swirls. Gray, nearly black, the water writhed out to sea in huge whorls, carving out the sandy banks. Now and then the oily flow was broken by a sluggish log or a fast-moving chunk of styrofoam. A casual observer might have mistaken the object that toiled there for such a bit of flotsam. Yet it moved strongly, with a purpose, and as it neared the southern bank its panting rose above the storm in a sharp series of fierce gasps, alarming in its compressed strength. At first the bank gave way under its struggle to emerge. For a moment it seemed on the verge of being swept out to sea until, with jaws capable of enormous leverage, it caught hold of the keel of a ruined boat embedded in the bank.

Jim drew himself up, hoisted his glass in preparation for a toast. "Maybe I don't have anything to say, but I want to say it all the same. Having had very little time or inclination to shop in these past weeks, I have some gifts to bestow in my own way, with the help of my late wife." Here he thrust up his chin with a broad smile, though emotion seemed about to engulf him. "Yes, a lot of what I want to say has to do with Joan." The name on his tongue sounded heartbreakingly lonely and forlorn. So many regrets. He had slowly come to realize that he had tried to leave Joan behind even while she still lived, but old loyalties were stronger than his own needs. He had tried to be an honorable man through those nineteen long years, when all but the first two had been painful and lonely ones. Joan, he wondered, what did I do to you? "Well," he said aloud, "on to the business of gifts."

"Dad, don't you think they should be saved till tomorrow?"

"I don't believe there's any precedent in that regard. What do you say, Judge?" He looked up at the stern, always disapproving portrait.

"He never believed in presents," Cathy said.

"Probably not," Jim conceded. "But, I have my reasons. Now you may find they don't fit, you may want to send them back. But first . . . oh, how like a lawyer . . . first, a few home truths." He dared a pause, staring from one to another.

Cathy groaned, and Bruce looked around helplessly. "Dad's summing up to the jury," she said, already apprehensive and embarrassed.

Jim would not be distracted. "This has been a strange, soul-searching month for me," he admitted, "and there are a few thoughts I'd like to get across to you, though I'm not sure I'm qualified to say them. I wonder all the time if Joan might still be with us if we hadn't tried so hard to cure her."

"Come on, Dad," Cathy protested, seeing disaster looming.

"No, Cat, don't reproach me, please. I've said that to myself more than you can imagine."

"Dad, can't we just let bygones be bygones?"

"Cath," he paused, closed his eyes, making them focus, "damn it, Cathy, they're not bygones, not yet. What I'm asking is, did Joan need medical curing or maybe just more loving? Or was it always hopeless? I mean, I have to wonder if some people aren't marked for self-destruction, no matter what. Maybe if I'd paid a few less experts and been a bit more caring . . . I know I wish I could tear up that marriage and start it over. More love, less medication."

Not knowing how he should react, Bruce sat listening in

167

a pose of false thoughtfulness. Cathy looked resigned; her father was into one of his hectoring moods and, like a storm, all she could do was wait it out. She wished she could escape into the kitchen and do the dishes.

"I think Joan was a victim of our tampering with her life," Jim went on. He wondered if similar manipulations had created the monster animals that had created so much fear in Sandy Cliffs. Would they ever really know what had been done at the Special Devices Research Center? The Mayor had still not received the promised written confirmation from the Center of the dogs' destruction. "I wonder, now, if I ever really listened to what she wanted."

There is for every living creature on earth a home, and the charred and snow-dappled beams of the Van Rath farmhouse had been that place. Uneasy, poised to run, the animal felt a kind of loneliness. Here it had been given its name, *Nachthund*. It had cared for the man, its teacher, and then the man had turned on it and its mates. It had no official existence, no identification beyond a code number in a closed file, but if any spot recalled the warmth of home it was here in this ruin. The creature's exploration was brief, the conclusion obvious: Nothing remained here. It lifted its head as if to howl, paused, and then the howl came, muffled, uncertain at first, for it had been trained to silence. The sound was almost like the sobbing of a child, and then the creature's eyes closed, its head went further back and the sound swelled in volume into a wailing shriek of despair and fury.

The call carried a long way, even in the snow-baffled air. All over Sandy Cliffs dogs, safe at their firesides, pricked up their ears. A few barked, to the consternation of their owners, who in one case turned on the front lights, anticipating carolers, but instead heard faint on the wind the eerie call that prickled the hairs on the back of his neck, a call that could have issued from the throats of the eternally damned or from their demon tormentors.

"Maybe I'm crazy," Jim said. "I know I'm not young enough anymore to know everything, but I know something's gone astray, something vital. Maybe there was no helping Joan, but those dogs. . . ." He shook his head. "I don't mean just those dogs, I mean applying knowledge without wisdom, I guess. We get rid of insects and end up killing eagles. Much more pollution, and you kids'll hear your kids say, 'But I thought snow was always black.' And what'll their kids say? Progress won't do us a bit of good if we're not here to enjoy it."

Jim was rolling now, rum-loosened statements that normally would have sounded deafeningly pompous in his own ears. "No more cold logic for me; it's all from the heart from now on, the way it always was for Joan." He stared at his daughter, seemed to sway forward, so intent was his gaze. "But you, Cat, you have a saving grace. You know how to laugh. If you can't laugh you're like gears without grease; you seize up. You can't adapt to changing times and not be changed in the process. Lord," he paused, "hear the old fool. . . . But, there's no stopping change or the pursuit of knowledge. Kings and dictators can't stop it and neither can the Church or the Communist Manifesto. Now if you want my opinion . . . oh, I know you're all bored stiff. . . . It's the *application* of knowledge that can kill you. Maybe one day, before it's too late, we'll get some respect for this planet. We'd better, or you'll all end up hiding, and then

169

you'll die. As for myself, I'm not quite done with living. If any of you had the good taste to ask me the reason for living?" He glanced around, eyebrows raised in question. "The reason is, to get ready to stay dead a long time."

Jim suspected he was making a fool of himself rambling on like this, but just then he felt in forgiving hands. "I don't think we come into the world with any promise it's going to be a picnic. Looking back, there's plenty to regret, and looking forward, there's a lot to fear, but that doesn't mean the bets are off. You kids have to take it from us, fill our places eventually. Now don't get the wrong impression; there's no rush. But be advised, the future can't do without the past any more than the other way around. Like it or not, we're your teachers, and I don't think we're very good at it. I'm not sure you're all that well prepared for what's coming up. And like it or not, Cat, you have years and years."

"I know," Cathy said, not looking at her father. "That's what scares me." It was as though the past, not even her own past, was a credit card with a catch phrase attached: As long as nothing went awry the debt could be paid off on a regular basis, but sooner or later, without warning, it would be foreclosed.

"Don't use your mom as an excuse, kiddo. You're too damned tough. Frankly, except for the way you look, I don't see Joan in you at all. The future can't scare the likes of Catherine Cooper. But I'm forgetting the point of this. It's high time I got back to the gifts. . . ."

Tireless, but with a curiously jarring pace, the creature trotted back the way it had come. On the beach the wind sang over the snow and sand. Ice crystals formed on the

170

creature's fur as it moved rapidly down the beach, its six-foot long silhouette seeming to enlongate with the swift and steady motion. From the beach it turned south, loping over the dunes and onto the ribbon of white road that cut through the meadow.

Jim raised his nearly empty glass. "Well, here's to the world, every crowded, polluted inch of it. And here's to the four of us, four absolutely unique people."

"To all of us," Cathy echoed. "And if we disagree, here's to me." She only touched the glass to her lips, had had almost nothing to drink, yet a faint skim of perspiration had appeared on her forehead. She remembered her mother at Thanksgiving. Either the room was too warm or the stresses of the evening were catching up with her.

"Without equals," Bruce toasted.

"Absolutely matchless," Jim added.

"Healthy and sober," toasted Pat, sipping significantly from her glass of seltzer.

"Sobering advice from one I much admire," Jim said, "and to her goes my first offering. My most selfish gift, undoubtedly too premature for good taste, but here it is: A proposal of marriage as soon as it may be seemly, with no strings attached. Only honest, unreserved devotion on my part." Jim paused, as if surprised by his own words. Astonishment was general. "The funny thing is, I mean every word of it." Still no response. "Even elephants get discouraged when nobody loves them. I need someone who needs me, or at least my money."

"Jim, you sound as though you're trying to tempt a hard-bitten chorus girl," Pat said.

171

"No, I always think of you as a farm girl, Pat. You turn out a fantastic apple pie."

"Jim, you know I burned that bridge."

"I know, Pat. I'm not trying to make you domestic. Sing where you want, whenever you want. No complaints so long as you're Mrs. James Cooper. Will you? Yes or no?" It seemed too big a thing for a simple yes or no answer, and none came. "It's not easy to plead one's own cause. Pat? Oh, I have done it now. Look at all your faces." Then more seriously, "Pat, I do need you."

"I know, Jim, and that frightens me." Pat stared at him with anxiety. One day, she felt sure, she would hurt him terribly. "Give me a little time to think, Jim," she added, looking into his eyes. In that moment neither spoke, and yet each told the other countless things.

"Strike one. Poor old Santa got himself stuck in the chimney that time," Jim said, and yet he did not feel discouraged. He had hope in what those eyes told him. They were, with the possible exception of Bruce's, the most honest ones he knew.

Where the meadow road turned west to follow the hill contours, the snow had drifted deep. Memory alone now guided the creature's steps and at the barrier of snow it slowed, then, horselike, gathered itself, going up and over like a dark wave. Beyond, the trees gave shelter and the unquiet inky shadows were filled with small night foragers, which froze to stillness at its passage.

23

▼▼▼

"Well, Bruce, you're next on my list," Jim explained. "You know, I simply have to look up at the mantle and that trophy there to know you're a winner." Embarrassed, Bruce studied his feet. "And when you've gotten this ocean race out of your system, and a B.A.—"

"That's a B.S., if you'll pardon me, sir," Bruce corrected apologetically.

"Whatever. If all else fails, I'll make you a deal: fifty-fifty in a charter boat business. How does that sound, coming from Scrooge on Christmas Eve?"

Bruce, who had been sitting trancelike, holding his grave young face in both hands, looked disbelieving but delighted. "You mean that, sir?"

"On my honor."

"Wow!" Bruce laughed but still looked bemused. His mouth stayed open a bit after the laughter. "I hope you're not kidding. . . ." The air was charged with emotion as

Bruce grabbed Jim's hand. "This is fantastic! You really do mean it."

Jim nodded; there had grown up a deep, instinctive liking between these two. Cathy found herself beaming, partly in encouragement, partly in delight. It really was becoming Christmas.

"Well, Dad," she said. "So you're a marshmallow after all."

"You know," Bruce interjected excitedly, "come summer, maybe the four of us could sail somewhere. Any suggestions?"

"Sure," said Jim. "The Galapagos."

"Terrific!" from Cathy. "Then on to Tahiti."

"New Zealand," Bruce offered. "The world!"

"I'm not sure I'm a good sailor," said Pat.

"It sounds impractical," Jim said automatically, but even as he mouthed the words he saw a sailboat on a lolloping ocean, islands rocking on the horizon in a blood-red sunset, and a faraway harbor glowing like a rope of diamonds. Then back to reality. "But I can see its possibilities. Now don't get me wrong, Bruce. This isn't a giveaway. I'm still a hard-bitten attorney, and rest assured I'd protect my investment."

"Still, I couldn't say no to an offer like that." Bruce stuck out his hand, and Jim's thrust out to grasp it. The intensity of emotion was almost embarrassing.

"All right," Jim said. "That's it for me, I guess. Time to trim the tree."

Near the Cooper woodpile, the creature that science had created took one puzzled turn around the snow-draped shepherd it had killed. This involved neither triumph nor

174

remorse, only curiosity, for it had no intention to do evil, though it had been deprived of any instinct to do good. It had been fashioned to endure everything beyond all imaginable limits of bone and flesh in order to haul down and destroy any unauthorized intruder in a given area. Unfortunately, those limits had never been fixed, so its prescribed territory was the world and all living things were its enemies.

Cathy sat up, ready to explode. "Well, what about me? What's my special present? Come on, Dad."

"I thought I was to save that for Christmas Day. But if you insist . . . mind you, it's not that spectacular. It's more of a lecture, really."

"Dad, get on to the present."

"Patience, Cat. Perhaps I should address you for the last time in the guise of Judge Cooper. I suspect you've already passed judgment on me, and now it's my turn. I call it: Thoughts on the merits of a good education. The gentleman over the mantle was the first to attend Princeton and Columbia, and three generations, not counting yourself, have gone to Berkshire. It's a tradition not lightly broken."

"One of us may regret this," Cathy said coldly. It was the same old record playing, and when he came to the part about boarding school Cathy meant to break it.

"Cathy, when I was your age I thought I knew everything. I was a fool. If you don't begin to have doubts after a few more years, you'll also be a fool. It's time to listen to my terms, Cat, my narrowed demands. Get yourself a decent education. You can't be overeducated. Wrongly educated, yes, but never overeducated. And when the time comes, at least consider law school. No need to look at me that way. I'm only saying consider it. I won't coerce you. You're old enough and bright enough to see the right and wrong of things. A good education in a good school, and you'll have enough flexibility to cope with this crazy world."

"What about Mom?"

"Cath, that's not going to happen to you. You may get run over by a car tomorrow . . . I can't predict the future. But you are most definitely not Joan. You're you, and just because the future's a question mark, don't let it scare you, kiddo. This is just the beginning. You probably have seventy years or more ahead of you. I'm just saying, use it well."

"Tell me another, Dad," she muttered under her breath. The future, the possibility that Joan's illness might lurk in her blood, still terrified her.

"You can do it if you try," he went on, as if he could read her mind. "I don't think I've ever lied to you, Cat. Get educated while you have me around to pay for it. A good education is the best defense, believe me."

"At home, Dad," she said stubbornly. "I want to go to school around here. I want to have a few friends for a change."

She waited for the ax to fall, but the moment never came. "I think that's fine," he said mildly. "All right, it's a deal. As long as you study hard," he warned.

It had all been so breathtakingly easy, Cathy found herself grasping for more. "Dad, could I start up the kennel again? Breed Taps for a start?"

"If you get on track with school, and I mean if, I probably won't say no. But it'll be a lot of time and work, and you'll have to sell most of the pups. I can't handle more than two dogs underfoot." He glanced down at Taps, who lay very flat on the floor with her ears tight against her skull as though expecting some punishment. "Look at her. She knows she ought to be out in the pen."

"Is that it, Dad? As long as I work?"

Jim nodded. "Which," he said, stretching, "tells me it's time to trim the tree."

"Dad, do you mind if we do more than that? I mean, sort of change a few things? Like that?" She gestured toward the painting over the mantle.

"Why not," Jim agreed. "He is kind of depressing."

So Judge Cooper came down and a watercolor of African animals took his place, a kind of Eden. "I never knew Mom did anything like that," Cathy said. "It looks like those paintings from Haiti."

"Outstanding, if you ask me," Bruce added.

The bonsai trees were banished to the study, and Cathy's old dolls took their place. It was a night they would never forget, yet one about which there was no final consensus. Reveille, dying as he had, would remain forever as Cathy's own tragic Beth Gelert. Yet good things had happened, too, hopeful things, and in this moment the Cooper household and their neighbors in Sandy Cliffs seemed to be snuggling down in the hollows of banked snow, their windows bright with the joy of the season.

At the kennel the creature paused again. Save for the torn wire, no sign of struggle remained. Yet it remembered the bullet that had stung its flank and the smell of the bitch in heat that had first drawn it there from so far away. Then a howl rose silently behind its closed jaws, as a comet might

177

howl through the empty void of space, or a stricken shark as it sank into the black depths of the sea.

Despite a lingering ache over Reveille and the aftershock of the attack in the kennel, Cathy felt for the first time in weeks a measure of contentment stealing over her. Maybe her father was right. There seemed to be such good cheer everywhere, in the sparkling ornaments, in the pine-scented air, just the four of them joined in honest affection in an infinity of time past and future.

"Shouldn't we tackle the tree?" she suggested.

"That we should, Cat," Jim replied as he ascended a stepladder. The others watched as they might observe an aerialist performing for the first time without a net. When he did not fall, they began handing up ornaments and instructing him where to hang them. At the end came the shabby angel with half her blond hair fallen out that had somehow found her way for so many years to the top of the tree, a soiled dove with bent wings, like a bathrobed and tattered refugee from the back streets.

"That was your mom's," he reminded Cathy as he put the angel in place. "You remember, it was her grand-parents'." And so the tree was complete, with a poor, mad angel at the top.

24

▼▼▼

Unmoving as an effigy cut from granite, it stood outside the radiant windowpanes. Its eyes were fixed on the scene, homicidal eyes that seemed to radiate light, as crazed as those of a bound eagle. Yet it was its nose that supplied what it needed to know. The bitch was still in heat, and she was there.

It was time for more carols, and while Bruce played the piano Pat took up the leather-bound book that bore the legend, "Leo Cooper to Sara, with abiding tenderness. Christmas 1893" inside the cover. She held it like the host before the altar, and as she sang Cathy noticed on Pat's face a different look; she was a detached visionary, doing the one thing she could do better than almost anyone else on earth. It could not have been a gift easily come by, either. Cathy had only to look at that pillar of a throat, slim yet singularly muscular. It was not simply something for a head to sit upon but a finely tuned musical instrument, painfully achieved. Yes, if I had a voice like that, Cathy thought, I wouldn't want to give up on it, ever.

They joined in, Pat leading the way, clear, right on key. Bruce frowned with concentration, absorbed in the music. When a carol ended, he asked, "Why doesn't Pat do a solo?"

Pat insisted she was just part of the chorus, though as the hymn progressed, even under restraint her voice rose gradually, capable of sustaining the high vaults of the melody. Jim only mouthed the words until he heard Cathy singing, in time to the music, "Dad's not singing, Dad's not singing."

The music stopped. "Why isn't he singing?" Bruce wanted to know.

"Because I can't carry a tune in a bedpan, if you want to know," Jim admitted.

"Dad, anyone can sing."

"You're asking for it," Jim warned. "Maestro, let's have "We Three Kings of Orient Are." It's gloomy, and I like it." His singing voice was deep and nasal, and intermittently Taps raised her head and howled along. The performance had them all laughing helplessly before he finished the final chorus.

From Jim's solo they proceeded in dutiful chorus to other mandatory carols, sung every year or it would not be Christmas. Cathy concentrated on the words until she noticed from the corner of her eye that Taps had moved away from the piano and now stood regarding the front windows, her whole body stiffened. As Cathy watched, Taps moaned softly. Cathy walked to the window, rubbed off the moisture with her hand and stared into the gray-white whirl.

180

"Cathy? What's the matter?" Pat asked from the other side of the room.

"Nothing," Cathy said. "I guess Taps heard something." The dog had returned to the rug in front of the fireplace, ready for a nap. "Let's do the "Twelve Days" again," she said. It was always the last and most necessary carol of Christmas Eve, and Bruce pounded away to the end. It left them breathless but laughing.

Then Pat said, "As far as I'm concerned, it's time for a few more presents, the old-fashioned kind—you know, wrapped up with paper and ribbons." She handed a small, bright parcel to Jim. "This one's a family thing." He praised the wrapping, held it to his ear and shook it, acting out a display of curiosity over its contents. It would be days before it was ever opened.

Bruce had left the piano bench, returned from the basement with more firewood. The rising flames reflected back from the black windowpanes, and Cathy thought she glimpsed Taps's image embalmed in the secondary glow. She was there at the window, all right, looking out, but that face in the glass was larger and as Cathy stared it seemed slowly to clarify like a print slowly developing in a darkroom tray. Perhaps because of the shadow, it seemed to be grinning.

"Cathy, what's wrong?" Pat exclaimed.

"It's there," Cathy said, anesthetized by terror.

The eyes behind the glass were not angry, not even threatening. Just cold, and waiting, like some force of nature. Cathy gestured toward them, made stabbing motions toward the glass with her finger. Then she screamed, and the scream was like a trigger as the glass exploded in-

181

wards—glass, dolls, snow, the storm window shattering like ice, and then the small inner panes with the wooden frames splintering. For an instant it poised on the sill, a dog the size of a pony, steel gray and beginning to bleed from the splinters, and then it was crouched, ready to hurl itself into the room.

25

▼▾▼

What happened in the next few seconds unfolded before Cathy's eyes with the shocking unreality of a traffic accident played out in slow motion. She saw that wide-open shaggy head filled with teeth haloed for one heartbeat by shards of glass. Then Taps unaccountably rose on her hind legs, meeting the onslaught, as the humans in the room scrambled out the door, which Jim slammed behind them.

Half a second more and that heavy partition jolted and rattled in its frame. Again it rattled before it seemed possible for the animal to have touched the floor, crouched, and leaped up again. The stout door banged a third, fourth, and fifth time as they forced the cluttered dining room table up against it. An overturned champagne bottle rolled frostily along the floor, but there was never a growl or bark from the creature itself, only the methodical pounding.

Cathy fled upstairs to her bedroom, slamming that door, too. She grabbed the phone, tapped out 911. Nothing. She tried again, realized there was no dial tone, and concluded in a fury that the phone downstairs must have been knocked from its cradle.

Sitting on her bed, the useless telephone still pressed against her ear, Cathy heard only silence while the cold of winter crept inside her clothes. She felt as though the walls of the familiar room were gradually closing about her. She breathed deeply, her eyes shut fast. This was how her mother must have felt, always, day and night, year after year.

Suddenly her eyes opened wide as she became aware of something just outside in the hall, something stealthy. She felt rising panic and then a kind of doomed apathy and resignation as the door burst open.

"My God, Cathy! We thought you'd been carried off!" It was Bruce, and she clung to him as to a life preserver. "It's all right," he assured her. "We're all fine. They've gone."

"They?"

"The two dogs, together."

"Taps went with that . . . went willingly?" She could hardly believe it.

"Looks that way."

Downstairs again, Bruce played a flashlight through the shattered glass, revealing branches of trees bowed lower and lower under their freight of snowflakes, which shone like iron filings in the beam of light. Also revealed were two sets of prints, heading away into the darkness.

"We ought to board that up," Pat said, but the only boards were outside on the woodpile, so in the end Cathy got a blanket, which Jim and Bruce hung from the curtain rod. Cathy tried the phone again, but it was still dead. The snow must have done something to the wires.

"Part of me wants to go to bed and pull the covers over my face," Jim said, "but I know I wouldn't be able to sleep." The problem would still be there to cope with later. He looked at Bruce to see if they were of one mind. They were agreed, all right, and the faces of both bore a look of fixed determination close to terror. Neither was the sort to seek violence of any sort, particularly to initiate it, but both felt resolved to act, obliged in what seemed now a very personal affair, as desperate and determined as gamblers who stake their last coins on one final draw. There would never be a clearer chance to bring things to a conclusion.

Their preparations for battle were undertaken with measured calm. Jim checked the action on the old Mauser, drove home the blue-black bayonet. One after another he pressed down the big brass eight-millimeter cartridges that seemed to give the rifle the proper weight of authority.

Bruce fed a handful of long rifle bullets into his .22. It held far more than the Mauser, but just how many it would take to stop the creature was open to debate.

"You're both crazy," Cathy said, and Pat, fixing on Jim, was insistent. "How can you be so irresponsible with another person's life?"

"It's my life, too," he replied.

"For God's sake, Jim!" Pat's hair was wildly disheveled; she looked like a crazed bacchante. It startled him to see the steadiest person he knew in such a state. They could not afford to become hysterical. Four lives were in his keeping and he must juggle with steady hands.

"Those tracks won't last long," he said.

"Jim, it's pitch-dark outside!" Pat yelled at him. "Bruce, what's the matter with the two of you?"

Jim was pulling on tall, black rubber Wellington boots.

Deliberately he drew on two wool sweaters, wound a heavy scarf around his neck, pulled on a ski cap. He was beginning to resemble a deep-sea diver. Finally came a heavy leather jacket.

"You'll get yourself killed!" Pat shouted.

"Dad, she's right." If they could stop Jim, Cathy knew Bruce would also give up the idea.

"Maybe," he admitted, "but what a hell of a way to go." Though Jim had reached an age when death no longer had a quality of fearful surprise, to be murdered on Christmas Eve just when life was looking up would be brilliant. "Look, I'm not going to waste time yammering with you while the tracks fill up with snow. I'm going alone if I have to."

"Jim, you're out of your mind. I'm calling the police," Pat retorted angrily.

"What for? They'll just arrive here in an hour and get their car stuck in the snow. Besides, the phone's dead, remember?" Fate had taunted him twice before tonight, at the kennel and again inside the sanctity of his own home. It was time to intervene and end this nightmare. This might be the last opportunity to be free of it, the beast that seemed determined to haunt them, with all the dark legacies of the past. He saw the hope of new beginnings. If he failed it would hang like an incubus around his neck and he might never shed his feelings of responsibility.

But the role of lonely hero was not to be. A precise, managerial voice that turned out to be Cathy's was saying, "Okay, I don't have a gun," and she marched into the kitchen and returned a moment later with two fearful weapons, a long triangular chef's knife and an even more fearsome cleaver. "Take your pick," she said to Pat.

186

"I'll probably stick myself in the foot with this thing," Pat said, grasping the cleaver. Cathy clasped the knife in her left hand, point downward, and picked up the flashlight with her right. "Okay," she said, "I'm ready. She felt so crammed full of fear and anger it seemed to ooze from her pores, making her sweat inside her down jacket.

"This is crazy," Pat said, a last protest as she hauled on her coat.

"Hurry," Cathy urged, thinking, my mouth said that. I didn't say that at all. Then she saw Bruce give a trembling yawn and she knew she was not the only one who was afraid.

Then they were out the front door, the two men with their rifles on either flank, Cathy and Pat in the middle. Their flashlights picked out the filling tracks in the snow, over which the wind sang a dry and lonely song. Stabbing at the icy air with her knife in practice, Cathy became aware of how inadequate a weapon it was, how weak her wrist. She felt like a dreamer, moving with the disembodied walk of slow stealth. Blood rang in her ears and she couldn't tell if the humming was inside or out. The snow moved across her vision in swift, blinding screens. The track, which led toward the development where Cindy Lawson had been found, was rapidly vanishing.

Through the snow she heard Bruce ask, "If I get a shot, where should I aim?"

Jim's first thought was, with that thing, I'm not sure it matters, but he replied calmly, "Just get 'em into him, fast as you can." At least Bruce seemed to handle the gun as if he knew what would happen when he pulled the trigger.

Here and there distant windows were bright with holiday colors. A car buried in a snowdrift winked its hazard lights:

187

Help, help. Drifts showed them where their quarry had plunged through, but the going was hard. The trail led through yards, over fences, past a row of four overturned and ravaged garbage pails. That was the first bit of luck, the first gain. From a house where no lights showed Cathy thought she heard a carol being sung at a funeral pace, well matched to her nightmare progress through the taffy-pulling drifts. On drawing closer she realized it was a dog lamenting the cold and his loneliness. Beyond there was only darkness: Trees and undergrowth, the thick belt of woods into which the Sound View development had been carved.

"Cath, where are you?"

"I can't see you," she protested.

"We're here."

"Wait, will you?" She stumbled on, the flashlight beam playing wildly like a small parody of searchlights sweeping London's sky during the Blitz.

She finally struggled through to the others. Why wouldn't they wait for her? "Not so much noise," Jim was saying, "and let's keep together." It wasn't her fault, she thought resentfully, that their legs were longer than hers. They moved on into a heavy shower of snow and momentarily lost the tracks entirely. Cathy cast her flashlight beam about, thinking hell must be white.

"There!" Pat called out, her beam playing on tracks that crossed a small, sluggish stream where lumps of ice floated in the licorice water like dead jellyfish. On the other side the brambles thickened. Cathy began feeling her way again as though blind and fell backwards in alarm when something thumped down beside her. She could vaguely see her father swing his gun around and realized some boughs had abruptly released their weight of snow.

188

The tangle of trees and underbrush suddenly gave way to the cleared swath of the housing development, where a water moratorium had brought construction to a halt. The two lights crept ahead, illuminating some finished structures. Other skeletal frames or cement foundations looked like so many white marble temples, a silent Bethlehem recreated under the gray, whirling dome of the stormy night.

Somewhere in the pit of her stomach it occurred to Cathy that the dogs might be curled up in any one of the half-finished houses, or crouched and peering down on them. "Oh, Lord," she murmured helplessly. The trail was lost again and her flashlight was developing an ominous orange cast. "Hurry," she commanded her legs, feeling the muscles in her thighs and groin beginning to ache in protest. Snow blew around her dense as smoke. She breathed hard and rapidly, a phantom traveling in the white plume of her own harsh exhalations.

She bumped into Pat in the darkness, grateful for the contact. Together they methodically played their beams over the snow-covered foundations. They followed the bulldozed road down through the trees toward the marsh, paused outside a half-finished house. No sign of tracks. Still Cathy could not absolutely free herself of the feeling that something was crouching inside. There was not a sound when she listened except for the wind, yet before entering Bruce pitched in a wet snowball. Finally Jim advanced with the bayoneted rifle, and the others followed, searching the ground with their yellow electric torchlight. Not a thing.

The next house was completed, to the extent of being locked, and there was no sign of a break-in. They went on, the wind mounting as they approached the open Sound. Snow flung itself into the beams of light at such a rate that

Cathy had a sense of hurtling forward at a reckless pace. She wanted to urge them all to slow down, to be more cautious lest they be taken unaware, but it was only a dog, surely, equipped at best with fangs, while her father held a rifle that might have killed men in battle. When it came to target practice, Cathy knew that Bruce was a good shot, too. Then why was she still so terrified?

They were all on edge. Peering into the next foundation, Jim suddenly raised his gun and fired. Even muffled by the snow, the concussion was stunning. "Damned fool, that did it," was his own comment. Whatever advantage they might have had by way of surprise had been squandered on a tar barrel. For a few minutes they rested, their backs against a finished wall where they could not be surprised.

By now at least half the foundations had been explored. They skirted the house where Cindy Lawson had been found. Almost finished, it had been padlocked and boarded up by police order to prevent morbid curiosity and vandalism. Not far beyond, Cathy thought she glimpsed a gliding shadow, little more than the winking of an eye. She could not be sure but on instinct called out, "Taps?" She whistled, got no response.

"I don't see anything," Bruce said, and the others agreed. Still a sense of increasing intrusion crept over her, proclaiming itself with a chill pain all around the lower rim of her stomach. She felt sure their every move was being observed and assessed. The conviction was so strong that Cathy could hear the creature breathing as though they wandered in the cavern of its gigantic lungs, lungs that drank in the enraging storm of human scent. She imagined its hot carnivorous breath on her cheek. Somewhere, just out of sight, it crouched in wait, mouth open. And then she saw the eyes, luminescent as though lit from within by some satanic flame. The eyes were there and then gone, so real and yet perhaps fashioned by her imagination out of chips of bottle glass left behind by a sloppy workman.

"You're right," Bruce said. "There's Taps." He pointed through the rush of flakes. "I think."

Cathy swung her flashlight in the direction indicated but saw nothing.

"Then he must be nearby, too," said Jim, and the sound of the rifle bolt cracking down was like someone snapping knuckle bones.

"How much time have we?" Cathy asked. She knew it was a stupid question, but she had to seek reassurance in the sound of her own voice.

"Now!" Bruce exclaimed as he stepped in front with his rifle leveled.

Somewhere a twig snapped, and Jim with a muffled curse drew back the bolt one more time to make sure a cartridge was in the chamber, shot the bolt forward again and down. Only then did Cathy see something behind a nearby foundation wall. It appeared at first to be a pumpkin or a large ball set upon the cement. At first she saw nothing alarming about it. The effect was so ludicrously unexpected that the reality developed only gradually with a welling up of terror too great to encompass all at once. "You!" she said out loud upon realizing that the creature was standing on the other side of the wall, looking over. To do that, it had to be gigantic.

To think it had been watching them all this time, complacent and confident, taking its time, even savoring the delay. With a rush, it might have been upon them in an instant.

191

Now it seemed content to wait; cunning, resourceful, without fear.

Jim raised his rifle again. "Come on! Come on, you!" he challenged, aiming as carefully as he could under the conditions. He had wasted one bullet already on a tar barrel, expended another in inspecting the magazine. Three remained. Without warning the rifle flashed and thundered, and as suddenly the head vanished from the wall.

"Got him!" Bruce exclaimed.

But Jim said slowly, "I'm not so sure."

They advanced on the wall cautiously. The flashlights disclosed fresh tracks. That was all.

"I don't think the batteries will last much longer," Cathy observed. There was an increasingly yellow quality to both beams, so evident that Pat's lamp was shut down for emergency use. Now they hunted with only one dimming eye. The conclusion was unanimous: They must head for home.

At first the decision seemed pure defeat, but once accepted it became gravitational. The idea of home, of light and warmth, propelled them, Bruce and Cathy in the lead, then Pat and Jim bringing up the rear, no longer the hunters but the hunted. By the time they reached the ice choked stream one light had given out entirely; the other pulsed dim as an ember.

Cathy kept glancing back. Nothing. Nothing but the snow. Then, yes, through the trees, emerging, then lost again, a moving shape, not so much approaching as gaining substance, like an object seen through smoky glass. At Cathy's cry they all turned in their tracks. A foundation wall intervened but hardly seemed to slow down the charge. The beast gathered itself and effortlessly cleared the barrier. The drifted snow scarcely retarded it.

192

Jim stood immobilized, a rabbit caught in the headlights of an onrushing car. Then he brought up the rifle. From the shattering explosion the attacker recoiled into a crouch, then came on again, silent as ever without fear of pain or death, something that might perhaps be destroyed but never hurt or discouraged.

Jim had barely time to work the bolt one last time, aim and pull the trigger. More shockingly audible than the expected shot was the dry click of a misfire. Then the dog rose, red gums showing above a mouthful of fangs. Forgetting the bayonet, Jim swung the gun like a club as he was flung backwards, then seized by the shoulder and somersaulted around in a cartwheeling universe. He tried to shove the creature away, the effort threatening to separate muscles from anchoring bones. He felt the hot breath from the devouring mouth upon his face and anticipated fangs cleaving his throat with annihilating agony.

More through terror than lack of it, Cathy stood her ground, steadily directing the weak beam of the flashlight so that Bruce might shoot if given the chance. It came when the beast stopped worrying the dark lump that was her father and advanced again. Then the little .22 discharged a dozen yelping shots, one explosion merging into the next, and still the creature moved with an unbroken stride as though drawn by the stream of bullets.

Crouching now beside Jim, Pat retrieved the Mauser from the snow, got off one clicking misfire, tried again. The gun bucked and boomed against her shoulder. The woods rang with echoes. The charging attacker was thrown sideways this time, but rose. A step in front of Cathy, Bruce clubbed his rifle. Only then did the great creature falter. It stopped, eyes still blazing in the reflected light, stood there, swayed. Though dripping with blood, its savage beauty held, its intent undiminished even by death.

Bruce had by now reloaded, but he did not fire. The creature simply stared at him from those yellow eyes, no longer vicious, but cold and sleepy, not hating, but as impersonally destructive as a tornado. It took one labored step forward. Bruce sighted the gun, but Cathy gently pushed the barrel down. "No more," she said.

Never having uttered a sound, it finally fell, its breath expelled in a mournful whistle as it hit the ground. The forelegs jerked once. A last spasm of nerves flickered across the fur.

Pat, then Cathy, knelt beside Jim. Bruce stood looking down at him, the rifle under his arm still oozing smoke from the muzzle.

Jim lay blood-spattered and still. Carefully Pat cradled his head. It was only then that he murmured, "Do I feel all right?"

"You tell us," Pat laughed with relief. "At least you're alive."

"If you say so," came the answer. A blinding headache assailed him as he opened his eyes on a gyrating world. He reached out a hand as he might toward an embodiment not quite real.

"How are you, Dad?" Cathy asked.

"Good question," Jim replied, trying to rise. His head felt full of broken glass. Then he noticed with alarm how his leg was bent nearly double. The anesthesia of shock, he cautioned himself, moving the leg gingerly to discover the tall rubber boot was half off his foot. Nothing seemed to be broken, though he felt incredibly shaken and sore. The blood that spattered his heavy leather jacket was not his.

No real damage except for his nose, which felt full of hot pepper.

"Not a thing, I guess, that won't wash off." Bruce gave him a hand up. "Thanks, old man. It looks like you saved my skin, or most of it."

"All our skins," Cathy said, "with a lot of help from Pat."

"That was one hell of a shot," Bruce said admiringly. "She's the one who stopped him cold."

This brought their attention back to the creature they had killed, and a moment of renewed alarm. If Jim were alive, why not that splendid, terrible animal as well? In the brief flutter of a cupped match, they saw the many punctures in its dark hide, the snow round about turning into dark slush from which Cathy uneasily removed her feet. It was mortal after all, and it could die, had to die.

"Well," Jim said, "I guess we made it, just barely." Man had gone too far in his tampering. Any further, and perhaps it would not be lying there but standing over their corpses, indestructible. Maybe the time had already come when a child, to survive, must be taught the remorseless, guiltless mentality of the psychopath. Perhaps the world called for such a messiah.

Cathy was cold and exhausted, trembling with terror's aftermath. There was no room in her head for such speculations. She only believed that most human beings were a little more decent than their circumstances allowed them to appear—most human beings, and their dogs.

"Does everyone feel like this afterward?" Cathy asked.

"How do you feel?" Bruce asked.

"Kind of sick."

"Me, too. And I've got the shakes. But I guess you have to be alive to feel this rotten."

"And I'm not sure why," continued Cathy, "but, well, ashamed."

The snow fell only intermittently, dusting the corpse, its huge head shattered, the great gaunt body riddled with wounds.

"Let's go home," Jim said. "I've got to let the police know."

"What do we do about her?" Bruce asked, referring to Taps, who had approached the other side of the corpse.

"Come on, girl," Cathy called out, pulling a leash from the pocket of her down jacket, but the shepherd responded with a low growl. "What's the matter, Taps?"

"She's guarding her mate," Pat said.

"Looks that way," Jim agreed. "She'll be home when she gets hungry. Let her be."

They had gone a few steps when Cathy looked back. Taps lay still in the snow, her nose touching the creature's corpse.

"Sure you can walk okay, sir?" Bruce asked.

"Just fine," Jim replied, though he could feel blood oozing under his hair.

"Let me carry the gun, at least. I don't want it said I didn't look after my partner."

The four went linked together in a laborious chain. The long nightmare was over. Lights seemed to welcome them back, bright Christmas lights.

Then it was Pat saying, "I may just be tired and overwrought, all this wild country living, Jim. I may come to my senses when the shock wears off," she rested her hand on his shoulder, "but I'm willing to give it a try."

"Marriage?" She nodded. "To me? Man and wife? The two of us?"

Pat gave him a quick bright smile. Cathy felt it rather than saw it there. "On terms described."

"It's a deal," Jim said, embracing her, a very domestic husband-and-wife embrace, more relief than passion.

Bruce went with his arm around Cathy's shoulder. She had seldom questioned that it belonged there, but now it seemed more permanent. Still, the future was long and uncertain, and she knew she was too young for such final decisions. Time would tell. Having survived this night, she felt they could survive most anything else the world threw their way. "Tomorrow and tomorrow and tomorrow," the words repeated in her head. There had been a time when she had thought otherwise. Now a stone had rolled away from her heart. All the days she lived from now on would be like those of Lazarus, a clear gain. She had survived her own death and she felt hovering around her the aura of a new self-possession.

The fear over being linked by heredity to her mother and therefore doomed was over, too; not past, not forgotten, but shorn from her future. Like the animal, Joan had been the victim of knowledge untempered by wisdom or sufficient love, but Cathy had survived them both. She had the confidence of one who has fought off a long illness, and she knew she was surrounded by people who cared.

No doubt Taps would return from her lonely vigil. If not, well, she would go back for her, bring Taps home. It seemed more than likely that Taps had been bred, would bear a litter spawned by technological excess; sixty-three days was the period for a dog's gestation. Cathy had no inclination to intervene or stop nature taking its course.

She no longer could accept the thought that bad qualities were inherited. Nature must have a way of healing itself despite man's interference. So let the pups be born. With any luck, Culloden Kennels might start out with something splendid and brand new, something good out of all that had gone wrong. Cathy knew she would probably have trouble convincing her father. She was no airhead, and if the savagery had been passed along with the excellence, Cathy never doubted she would know and be tough enough to do what had to be done while the pups were small. Strangely, this did not trouble her. The great fear had lifted. Her allegiance was with the future, not the past.

It had been a close shave, but it was not the end, not Armageddon or the final ice age. She felt herself tougher now. She had the front teeth to hang on with, and as long as she hung on, what might seem the end would mean only new beginnings, though perhaps not the beginning of exactly what she wanted. Take the present one day at a time, each one a miracle, simply getting up in the morning, meeting people, learning, eating something different, finding a bit of laughter, loving someone. How amazing all that was. And Christmas . . . how beautiful was this season of reaching out, even if it did not mesh with the fierce realities of the year crowded around it. Every year over the centuries it came again, a kind of reaffirmation of humanity. She believed that now and felt she always would.

"Dad, I never did exactly say thanks for that present. I want you to know I intend being one heck of a student from now on. Maybe even a law student."

"Maybe even a judge," Jim replied.

"Maybe," she agreed. "Anything's possible." And it seemed to Cathy without doubt that anything was indeed possible so long as she was willing to make the effort.

Ahead through the occasional falling flakes was the Cooper home. Through shredding clouds stars flashed signals and like a solitary red ornament in the driveway a police car blinked on and off. A shovel crunched lugubriously.

"I suppose it's the chief," Jim said. "With this snow, he'll be our guest for the weekend."

"I'll make him chocolate chip cookies," Cathy said. She sensed this night there was happiness everywhere, like the oxygen in the air she breathed. Hanging on Bruce's arm she said, "Let's cheer him up. Let's give him 'God Rest Ye.'" And so they broke into the old carol, the four of them stumbling down the drive. The last big snowflakes fell into their open mouths. Flakes fell on the Sound, disappearing into the blackness there, and onto the jagged ice heaped along the shore. The tapering snow fell on the houses that sparkled with Christmas cheer and upon houses that were dark and unfinished, upon the thick woods and upon a dog that stood like the living cast of a mad victory. The end precedes the beginning, and the end and the beginning are always there waiting, before the beginning and long after the end.

"God rest ye, merry gentlemen," they sang to the policeman stuck in the drive, "let nothing you dismay."